the Ballad of Carson Creek

the LONE WOLF

Part 1 : FEARLESS FLYERS

by

James Russell

Visit
balladofcarsoncreek.com

For Samantha.

Table of Contents

Prologue
'A Cold House'

Thursday, December 28th, 1944 - Age 5

"C'mon, Huey!" Gary called, struggling to step through the eighteen inch blanket of snow, which rose well past his knees. He drew a shiny silver whistle from his coat pocket and blew it.

Huey, a small, sand-colored mutt, resembled a dolphin as he bounded across the field, porpoising in and out of the snow, his ears perked and his tongue flapping in the frigid air. Gary continued his trudging toward the hill's tree-lined crest, still some fifty yards ahead. All he could think about was how much fun it would be to sled ride down the hill he was climbing, hoping desperately that he would receive a new sled for his birthday, since his mother had already run over the one he'd been given for Christmas with the car.

The dog finally caught up with him, muzzle caked with snow.

"And you can sled down with me, Huey," Gary said, patting the pup's head. "We could go *real* fast then!"

At last, his cheeks flushed and his nose rosy and running, he reached the top of the hill and the landscape opened up before him; miles and miles of rolling, snow-covered countryside, sparsely dotted with homes and barns, all nestled among the bristling patchwork of winter-whipped trees. The sun seemed to rest on the flaming western horizon.

Gary, the radiant glow of the sunset painting him orange, brushed the snow off a tree stump and sat down, letting out a deep breath. The vapor drifted away slowly, catching the light. He exhaled again, this time directing the cloud as if he were smoking a cigarette, like all of the adults he knew. He was, after all, going to be six years old in just four days, and he thought he'd better start practicing for adulthood.

Huey whined softly and laid his head in Gary's lap.

"S'matter, boy?" Gary asked, stroking the pup's head. His gaze turned to his house below, resting at the bottom of the field amid a patch of gnarly, naked oak trees. He watched as a thin wisp of smoke lazily snaked out of the chimney and into the twilight sky. "Know what I wish? I wish I had a brother to play with." He turned to the dog and added, "Not that you ain't fun to play with, Huey, I just wish I could have another human being to play with, too... Mama says I'll have to wait till Daddy gets home from the army." His thoughts drifted from having a human playmate to an image of his father holding a rifle in one hand and an American flag in the other, shooting away at the bad guys, whoever they were. His mother had mentioned that he was on an island somewhere, so he imagined all of this taking place on a sandy, sun-drenched beach, with turquoise waves splashing up in the background. His father was his hero. He wanted to be just like him when he grew up, which, in his mind, was something that was rapidly approaching.

His thoughts continued to dance between what being a six-year-old would be like, to his father, to how much faster it would be to get home if his mother was a more adept driver and hadn't crushed his new sled, and finally to his rumbling stomach. It was getting dark, and his mother hadn't blown her whistle yet. That meant he still had time to play. But he was hungry, and becoming cold just sitting on the stump.

"Well, boy..." he said, slowly standing up, "You ready for some supper?"

Huey's ears perked up and he began wagging his tail frantically.

"I'll race ya home!" Gary yelled, taking off down the field, with the dog quickly catching up and overtaking him, barking excitedly. Running wasn't really an option due to the deep snow, so Gary shuffled as quickly as he could, following in Huey's wake.

Huffing and puffing, he finally reached the creek at the bottom of the hill and very carefully began traversing the slippery, snow-covered log that served as a bridge to his backyard. He spread his arms out for balance.

Below, Huey splashed through the gently tumbling brook and up through the cattail stalks on the opposite side, stopping to shake off the freezing water.

"Wait for me, boy!" Gary called. Not without a few hairy missteps, he eventually made it across the log bridge and into the back yard, where he began trudging toward the large, gray farmhouse he called home. There weren't any lights on in the windows, which he thought was peculiar, given that the sun had now fully disappeared behind the trees and had left only a fleeting glow in the west, but he continued onward, not thinking any more of it. Upon reaching the house, he slowly ascended the icy front porch steps, hanging on to the handrail so not to slip, and walked up to the front door and stomped the snow off of his boots.

"Stay," he pointed to Huey, who trotted over to a blanket in one of the partially enclosed porch's corners and laid down. "I'll bring your supper out after a while." Gary turned the knob and pushed the door open.

The house was dark, as he had seen from outside, and a slight chill hung in the lemon-scented air. Usually, some pleasant, warm aroma would be wafting from the kitchen, but not this evening. He glanced up at the coat rack, where, sure enough, his mother's coat hung, and her snow boots sat below it. She hadn't gone anywhere.

"Mama?" he called out, stepping into the living room. The old radio in the corner was softly filling the area with Bing Crosby's *'I'll Be Seeing You'*, and he noticed that the Christmas decorations, the ones his mother had said earlier she was taking down, still hung on the door frames and stair railing, along with the dilapidated tree sitting in the corner, silver tinsel feebly clinging to its predominately bare, sickly branches. He pulled his stocking cap and scarf off and tossed them on a chair, and then walked into the dinning room, where the only thing set out on the table was a half empty bottle of bourbon and an overflowing ashtray. He continued to the kitchen and switched on the light. Nothing in the oven, nothing on the stove, and no sign of anything having been in either place. A bowl of oranges sitting on the counter was the only food in sight, so he took one. He strode over to the basement door and opened it. "Mama?" he called down the dark, musty stairwell. The lights were off. Clearly, she wasn't in the basement.

Retracing his path back into the living room, he slipped out of his heavy coat and laid it with his hat and scarf. He began peeling the orange as he headed toward the staircase, placing the bits of peel in his overalls pocket. As he took the creaky steps one by one, the air temperature began dropping considerably, and if it hadn't been so dark, he probably could have seen his breath. What was going on here? he wondered.

"Mama?"

He reached the second floor and immediately felt a chill breeze hit him. It seemed to be coming from the door directly across from the stairs, which was slightly ajar. It led to the bathroom. He took a few steps closer. A very faint shaft of light, natural light, presumably coming in through the bathroom's large window, passed through the narrow crack and cut across the landing's carpet at an angle.

"Mother?"

Silence. He pressed his hand against the door, opening it with a slight push. It felt like he'd stepped in to a freezer. And there she was. Silhouetted against the large, partially open window, she was reclining in the claw foot bathtub, her head laid back against the rim, her arms resting on the edges. The soft white light that filtered in through the sheer curtains created a halo about her. She must be sleeping, he thought.

"Mama!" Louder this time.

She didn't stir, so he moved closer. He noticed an empty glass tumbler sitting on the floor beside the tub, ice cubes still intact. And then he saw the dark rivulets that had trickled down the side of the tub and into the bath water, dribbling from two gaping wounds in each of her forearms. A bloody-edged straight razor sat on the window sill. He dropped the half-peeled orange he'd been holding and his heart instantly began to pound against his chest.

"M-M-Mama...?" Tears began to well up in his eyes. He reached for her arm and shook it gently. Her skin felt like chilled glass. When she didn't move, he shook her again, harder this time, frantically. Her head rolled toward him. Her soft, brown eyes were open, staring past him, her mouth parted slightly. Her naked body was pale and bluish, contrasting against the dark, blood-tinted bathwater.

Gary's tears began to stream faster. He shook her a third time, with both hands. "Mama, wake up!" He knew she wasn't sleeping, he was smart enough to know what had happened, but he didn't want to accept it. He drew his hands away. They were covered in blood. He began wailing uncontrollably, wrapping his arms around her head and pulling her close, crying, "*Mama, Mama, Mama...*" Tears fell from his face to hers.

Gary was awakened by Huey rustling beside him. It

took him a moment to recall why he was sleeping on the barn floor, curled up in a nest of scratchy straw, freezing in just his sweater. Then he remembered, and wished he could just go back to sleep forever and forget all about everything. He felt more lost and alone than he ever imagined possible. Wiping away a fresh crop of tears, he laid his head back down in the straw and watched the dust float through ribbons of morning sunlight that pierced through the gaps in the barn wall. How could this happen? Why? The sorrow felt like an anvil sitting on his small chest.

Huey stirred again, and then sat up, ears perked. He let out a loud bark and took off through the partially open barn door.

"...Gary!" called a slightly hoarse voice from outside. It sounded like his grandfather.

Gary sat up.

Against the blaze of the sunrise, the silhouette of a man, tall and wearing a fedora, filled the doorway. "Gary?" The man pushed the door open further.

Gary, shivering, squinted at the light now cast upon him. "Grampa Roy?" he choked.

The man began to cry, kneeling down on one knee and opening his arms to Gary. "Come here, son..."

Gary jumped up and ran to him, burying his face in his grandfather's chest, bawling.

"I know, boy... I know," Roy said, holding Gary tight. They cried together in silence for a few moments. Finally, Roy sniffed and stood, removing his heavy wool coat. He draped it over Gary's shoulders and then lifted him into his arms.

Gary remained quiet, laying his head on his grandpa's shoulder and closing his eyes tight, squeezing out the tears.

"Come on, let's get you warmed up."

"I... I don't want to go in the house..."

Roy stepped out of the barn and began high-stepping across the large, snowy back yard. "That's alright, Gary. You can wait in the car. I'll have granny get you some clothes from your room."

Gary opened his eyes, seeing for the first time several police cars and an ambulance sitting in front of the house. He saw his grandmother on the porch, speaking to a policeman. When she caught sight of him, she came running as fast as her elderly legs would allow, her silver hair floating in the slight breeze.

"Gary!"

Gary wiped his face on his sweater sleeve and let Roy lower him to the ground. He met her with an embrace.

"Oh, Gary, dear..." she wept, "where have you been?" She brushed some straw out of his hair. Gary held her tight, not speaking.

"I found him in the barn. He needs some warm clothes."

"I'll go get you some, dear," she said, releasing Gary. "Go wait in the car, I won't be a moment." She started back for the house.

When Gary didn't move, Roy took him by the shoulder and led him to the burgundy Chevrolet. "Come on, son. Grandma Kate will get your things."

Gary stopped and turned around. "Huey..."

"I'll find him. He can come, too. Go on, get in." Roy opened the sedan door. "We'll leave shortly."

Gary got in. He curled up on the back seat, pulling Roy's coat over him like a blanket.

Soon, his grandparents returned, along with Huey, who jumped up on the seat beside him. The pup began licking Gary's face, which was still streaked dark red from wiping away tears with bloody hands.

Roy turned the key and pointed the car toward the long lane that led from the house to the road.

"Where are we going?" Gary finally spoke, sitting up.

Kate turned to face him, her watery blue eyes full of sympathy and sadness. "We're going home, dear. You'll be staying with your grandfather and me for a while. Alright? Everything is going to be okay." She tried her best to smile through her tears.

Gary craned his neck to look out the frosty back window. How could anything ever be okay ever again? he thought. He watched the old gray farm house slowly disappear behind the snowy pine trees that lined the curving lane.

"Are you getting warm, sweetheart?"

Gary turned back toward her and heaved an exhausted sigh. He put his arm around Huey and laid back down on the seat, trying his best not to start crying again. No amount of heat could chase the cold that had settled in his heart.

Chapter 1
The New Frontier'

Saturday, July 8th, 1949 - Age 10

The milky full moon glow found its way through the open window and into Gary's small bedroom, rippling across his blanket as it cut between the leaves of the large, gently rustling maple tree just outside. The faint breeze served only to carry in the cicada song, from a choir of thousands, and did very little to quench the oppressive heat of the night. Gary let out a sigh. He sat with his back against the wall, wide awake, eyes transfixed on the small alarm clock that seemed to be mocking him from the nightstand. It was nearly 4:00am. He wiped his sweat-speckled forehead on the shirt he'd stripped off hours ago and tried to lay back down. Useless. After a few more minutes of tossing and turning, he sat up again, growling slightly. He needed to get some fresh air.

Mind made up, he scooted off of the bed and tiptoed across the wooden floor, so not to wake his grandparents below, and quietly tugged open his dresser drawer, pulling out a pair of jeans and a shirt, which he slipped on, and then dug through the various other garments to the bottom of the drawer, where he uncovered a .45 caliber pistol. He stuck it in his waistband and turned toward the open window.

It didn't take him long to cross the narrow stretch of slate roof and jump the three foot gap to the tree. The branch creaked slightly beneath his weight. He froze, holding his breath, praying silently that he hadn't been heard. The last thing he needed was to get caught sneaking out of the house; he was already in enough hot water after giving Fred Edwards a black eye yesterday. Although, he hardly saw how he was to blame. He hadn't wanted his grandmother to invite Fred over to play in the first place. She just couldn't understand that he was much happier being alone, and that he had no desire to be friends with anyone. He'd made it this far in life without them. Why couldn't it stay that way?

He wrapped his arms and legs around the tree and quickly scampered down to the yard, landing in a crouched position just outside his grandparents' window, where he stopped again, listening. Grandpa Roy was snoring. So far, so good. He remained hunched over as he walked along the yellow farmhouse to the back porch, where he found his muddy rubber high-top boots that had been permanently banished to the outdoors.

"Damn," he muttered softly, using the only curse word he'd ever heard his grandfather utter. He'd forgotten to bring socks. Picking up the boots, he overturned them, dumping out all manner of dirt, rocks and other earth matter, and then reluctantly pulled them on his feet. With that, he adjusted the gun in his waistband and took off for the field.

As he passed by the barn, Huey, tail wagging frantically, ran to join him, whimpering softly as Gary stooped down to pet him.

"Shhh... Quiet, boy. Let's go see our hideout..."

The field was teeming with life; birds, frogs, crickets, cicadas, all joining together in a grand natural symphony. The full moon's glow blanketed the countryside in white, making it easy to navigate, and Gary, with Huey trotting along at his side, opted to take a path that ran next to the gently tumbling, tree-lined creek that snaked its way through acres and acres of thigh-high corn.

"Boy, is it hot out here," he said to himself, leaning down to pick up a short stick. He flung it away, hissing, "Go get it, Hue!" The mutt shot off running through the weeds. Gary, gazing up through the tree canopy to the starry sky, rested his hand on the pistol's handgrip. His thoughts turned to his father. The gun was the last thing he'd given Gary before disappearing into a rainy March night three years ago, reeling in a drunken stupor, giving no indication as to where he was going or when he'd come back. Gary was beginning to doubt that he ever would. In fact, he was beginning to doubt if he was even still alive. His grandparents were adamant that he was not to blame for both his mother and father's behavior, but he still couldn't help but think that there was some reason that he'd been abandoned. His musings were interrupted by

Huey, who came running back with what looked like half a rabbit dangling from his jaws.

"Hey, that's not what I threw," Gary said, wrinkling his nose at the pungent odor rolling off of the dead animal. He pointed to the ground and snapped his fingers. Huey dropped the corpse.

Before long, he cut east, maneuvering through the rows of corn as the earth rose in a steady incline for several hundred yards, ending where the field butted up against a heavily wooded crest. He located a narrow, almost invisible path that cut through the trees. Wading into the overgrown thicket, gingerly pushing thorny blackberry branches out of his way, he continued to trudge upward until the wooded hill's ridge began to level out and then, shortly afterward, drop off into a small, bowl shaped depression.

"Here we are, boy," he said, sliding down the bare, root infested wall and into the grassy little hollow. Huey scampered down behind him. He wasted no time in making his way across to the clearing's lone tree, a gnarly, decrepit pear, where he reached into a hole in the trunk and drew out a large, glass Mason jar. Taking it in both hands, he walked to a nearby log and sat down. He pulled the pistol out of his waistband and laid it beside him, and then grasped the dirty, yellowed, spiderweb-spangled jar and began to open it. It took a bit of grunting effort to loosen its rust-encrusted lid, but, finally, it broke free and twisted off.

Reaching inside, he first drew out a half empty pack of Chesterfields and a book of matches that he'd 'borrowed' from his grandfather's workshop. His head began to buzz slightly as he lit one of the cigarettes and inhaled, stifling a cough. After puffing for awhile, he stuck his hand back into the jar and pulled out a harmonica, which he blew into once and sat down in his lap. More rummaging yielded a toy car, a few silver dollars, a gold tooth, some fancy marbles, a medicine bottle full of whiskey, his old silver whistle and a handful of bullets for his gun. Finally, all that remained was a tiny, lace-trimmed handkerchief that had been knotted into a ball. Almost hesitantly, he brought it out and sat the jar at his feet. It took him a moment to untie the knot. As the corners began to fold open, they revealed a thin, silver, diamond ring nestled in the silky fabric. The stone was small, but sparkled vibrantly as Gary lifted it up, casting dancing speckles of moonlight across his face. It was his mother's wedding ring. He'd stolen it from his father's bureau after hearing him talk of selling it to pay off some 'old debts', which, Gary knew all too well, translated to 'booze and craps'. He wasn't having that. He had few memories of his mother as it was, nothing more than a handful of fleeting images and feelings; her tender, sad brown eyes, the softness of her fingers when she would cut his hair, the way she greeted him when he returned home from school... Grandma Kate had tried to explain to him that Evelyn was a very sick woman, and had she been fully aware of her actions, she never would have left him. He tried not to think about it too much. As he gently placed the ring back into the handkerchief, an old, familiar feeling of heartache began to grow in his chest, accompanied by a lump in his throat. He squelched both away, hastily tying the ring up and dropping it back into the jar at his feet, dumping all but the harmonica back on top, as if burying it away. Smashing out the cigarette, he brought the harmonica to his lips and began to play.

Hours passed, and soon the sun began creeping up

over the horizon, sending beams of golden heat through the trees around him. It was time to start heading home. But just as he was about to drop the harmonica back into the jar, he heard a branch snap. Huey, who had been laying at his feet, perked up and growled softly, sniffing the air in the direction of the path. Gary's hand unconsciously reached for the pistol. The rustling continued to move closer. As his fingers snaked around the handgrip, he was reminded of the black bear tracks he'd encountered earlier that week on one of his excursions. He really didn't want to fire shots off this early in the morning, but getting mauled by a bear was not on his to-do list for the day; that would be far worse than getting caught sneaking out of the house. He held his breath, preparing for the worst. Fortunately for him, black bears didn't have red hair and wear dresses. It was Margret Henchy, a neighbor of the Bells, whom Gary had become somewhat acquainted with on his many egg deliveries. She was the only girl he'd ever really spoken to at length, and he'd nearly tried to kiss her once, but choked at the last second, given the fact that she was a year older than him and several inches taller. Plus, she was kind of pretty.

"Maggie?" he said, putting the gun down.

"Gary Bell... I thought I heard music up here." She slowly climbed down the side of the hill, trying not to soil her navy blue dress. "What are you doing up here?"

"Uh," Gary dropped the harmonica in the jar. "What are *you* doing up here?" He was perturbed by the fact that someone, no matter how pretty, now knew where his secret hideout was.

Maggie reached down and patted Huey on the head, and then walked over and sat down beside Gary, straightening her dress. "I was milking Daisy and heard music. I'd seen you come up here before, so I figured it was you."

"Oh..." Apparently, he hadn't been as careful about his hideout as he'd thought...

"So what are you doing up here?"

"Oh, nothin'... I just wanted to go for a walk."

"Why do you have a gun?"

"Umm... protection."

"From what? What's in the jar?"

"Just stuff." Gary picked up the jar and pulled it to his chest.

"Like what?"

"Like... just some of my stuff."

She leaned in closer. "Is that a silver dollar in there?"

"Uhh... Maybe." She was close enough for Gary to smell her shampoo. It smelled fresh, like clean linens. He noticed his hands trembling slightly.

"Can I see?"

As much as he wanted to stay and chat, he really needed to get her out of there and make it home before his grandparents realized he'd been gone. He quickly reached in and dug out one of the coins. "See?"

Margret held out her hand. "I want to hold it."

Gary sighed and placed it in her open palm. "Look, I really need to get going, Maggie..."

"What's your hurry?"

"Well, my Grandparents don't know I'm up here and... and I don't want them finding out about this place."

"Ohhh..." Margret smiled, wrinkling her freckled nose. "I see..."

"So it'd really be great if you didn't say anything to anybody. It's... it's supposed to be a secret."

"Well..." She tapped her chin, mulling over something in her mind. "I'll make you a deal."

Gary groaned. "Like what?"

"I'll keep your secret. Forever. But you have to give me this." She held up the coin.

"Wait a minute, no way!" Gary shook his head, standing. "No way a secret is worth a dollar!" He began pacing in front of her. Hush money wasn't something he was used to paying.

"Well, then I guess you're going to have to find a new hiding spot."

"C'mon, Maggie... I... I thought we were friends!" As much as he didn't like people, he didn't mind being friends with girls. Or at least imagining he was.

"So did I."

"Then why..." Gary stopped and thought for a moment. Maybe he could kill two birds with one stone. "Okay, but I want something else, too. A dollar is too much for just keeping a little, tiny secret like this."

Margret furrowed her brow. "What else do you want?"

Somehow, asking this way, Gary didn't feel quite so nervous. "I want... I want a kiss."

"What?" she exclaimed. "Are you serious?"

"Yep."

"But we're just friends, Gary! And you're only in fifth grade!"

"I know, but it wouldn't be like a *'love'* kiss... Just a... I just wanna know what it feels like..."

Margret looked down at the silver dollar. "I don't think-"

"Just a real quick one. And you get to keep the dollar. Forever." Gary gulped. He was beginning to lose his nerve.

"Well..." She continued to flip the coin around in her fingers. Finally, after what seemed to Gary like minutes, she slipped it into her dress pocket.

Before he could talk himself out of it, and before she could stand, he bent down and planted his lips on hers, bending her backward. She seemed to struggle against him for a moment, but then settled into the kiss, putting her hand on the back of his neck and kissing him in return. All of his wondering was over: it felt good. Better than anything else he'd ever experienced, like his brain was joyously celebrating the Fourth of July inside his head. He didn't want it to end, but he'd promised a quick one, so he began to pull away. Maggie reeled him back in.

They kissed until Gary's mouth hurt. When he finally stood up straight, his back was aching, but he didn't care.

Margret's brown eyes fluttered open. "Gary..." she said quietly, "where'd you learn to kiss like that?"

Gary licked his lips. "Uhh... the movies." He could scarcely believe it. He'd finally kissed a girl.

"I've never been kissed like that before..." She stood, hand on her cheek, looking somewhat smitten.

"Was it worth a dollar?" He suddenly felt a bit taller, a little more grown up, mature. He knew right then and there that his new life goal was to kiss as many girls as humanly possible.

She smiled, giggling slightly. "Yes..."

"Okay, then give it back."

"What...?" she asked, confused.

"You said it was worth a dollar, so give me my dollar back."

"But, Gary, you said..."

Gary broke into a smile. "Aww, I'm just teasin'. But if you tell anyone about this place I *will* burn your house down."

Margret didn't know whether to laugh or run.

Gary stuck out his hand. "Deal?"

She slowly accepted his handshake. "Gary, you are one of the strangest people I've ever met..."

"Thank you. Now run along, I gotta hide my stuff."

She stood up and began walking away backwards. "Okay... 'bye..."

Gary screwed the lid back on the glass jar. He now had a mission in life, and he couldn't wait to get started. Tossing a cocky, "Yeah, see you around, kid," over his shoulder, he began making a mental list of all the kissable dames he knew. Girls... they were the new frontier.

Chapter 2
'Pals With Gals'

Tuesday, September 20th, 1949 - Age 10

Gary's fist was far too large to fit up Ernie Spencer's nose, but that didn't keep him from trying with all of his heart. Again and again, he buried his balled-up hand in the boy's face, until both of them were spackled with specks of rosy red blood. Gary's breath came hard. He did his best to hold back the tears that had begun to well up in his eyes, or at least hide them from the fifteen or so children encircling the brawl. His ears were ringing so loud that their shouts were apparent only by their wide open mouths and pumping fists, pumping in unison with his. He kept swinging. Weeks of pent-up anger fueled every punch, and sixth-grader Ernie Spencer, whom he was now sitting on, just happened to have been the straw that broke the camel's back. Swing, swing, swing. Ernie was beyond fighting Gary off; he just lay there in a daze, nostrils streaming blood like tiny faucets. Gary seemed possessed, on a mission, and if it hadn't been for the firm arms of his school teacher wrapping around his chest and pulling him off of Ernie, permanent damage would no doubt have been inflicted.

"Gary Bell!" she yelled in his ear, struggling against his writhing, flailing body. "Stop this this instant!"

Gary tried unsuccessfully to lunge away from her, grunting through his tears. He finally stiffened, gasping for breath while his eyes roved wildly over the now silent crowd that encircled him, and then fixed on Ernie's limp, unmoving form. He spit on him. The next thing he felt was the back of Miss Lloyd's hand.

Principal Martens just shook his head, running his fingers through his slicked, black hair. "Gary, Gary, Gary..." He let out a deep sigh, and then leaned forward, resting his elbows on the large mahogany desk. "What are we going to do with you?"

Gary, sitting across from him, stared at his knuckles for a moment, and then wiped his running nose on the back of his hand. He didn't really care what they were going to do with him. His apple green eyes finally locked on to the principal's weary gaze, but he remained silent.

"Don't you have anything to say for yourself?"

No. He didn't.

Martens sighed again, leaning back to open one of his desk drawers. He drew out a long wooden paddle and laid it in front of Gary. "What were you boys fighting about?"

Gary held his gaze, not even glancing at the paddle. "He was saying things about my family."

"What kind of things?"

"Mean things. Bad things. He said that my mother was a whore and that God made her kill herself for it."

Principal Martens' eyebrows rose slightly. "He said that? Exactly?"

Gary nodded. "And he's said other things before. Lots of kids have."

"How often? Gary, you should have told your teacher."

"All the time. People make fun because I live with my Grandpa and Grandma and because I don't have a real family. Even kids in older grades, like Ernie."

"Gary..." Martens rubbed his temples. "Why haven't you told anyone? Violence is no way to solve these types of problems."

"Yeah? I'll bet he don't do it again."

"Well..."

"I'm not sorry about it. He had it comin' to him. I'm not gonna say I'm sorry." Gary finally glanced down at the paddle. "So I guess you can just whip me now."

Martens closed his eyes for a moment, and then reached for the paddle. "Gary, if you keep taking matters like this into your own hands, you're going to put me out of a job. Discipline is one of my duties..." He stood up and walked over to the bookshelf that sat in the corner. "Now I know that things have been difficult for you at home lately," he said, pulling a large, leather-bound book out of its place. "And I know what it's like when people say hurtful things to you." He reached for an old brown coat, which hung on a rack beside the bookshelf, and then turned to Gary, lowering his voice. "But if these brawls don't cease, I am going to be forced to punish you. Do you understand?"

Gary nodded slowly. He watched, curious, as the principal laid the book down on his desk chair and then draped the jacket over it. He raised the paddle, along with his voice.

"Mr. Bell, let this be a lesson to you!" He brought the paddle down hard on the book, twice. *Whap! Whap!* "I expect this behavior to cease once and for all!" *Whap!*

Gary, eyes wide, watched the dust billow out of the old coat with each blow of the paddle.

"Next time the punishment will be greater!" *Whap! Whap! Whap!*

Gary's mouth hung open. He was stunned.

Principal Martens laid the paddle on the desk and motioned for Gary to stand. He then crouched down, looking him directly in the eyes, whispering adamantly, "This won't happen again, Gary, do you understand? If you have a problem with anyone, no matter who, you come directly to me."

"Y-yes, sir..." Gary whispered back. Martens put his hand on Gary's shoulder.

"Good. Now look sad for my secretary." He stood up straight and opened the frosted glass door for Gary, winking.

Gary felt a smile tugging at his lips, but he forced it back into his best frown. Passing by Mrs. Rokissian, the school secretary, he rubbed theatrically at imaginary tears, avoiding her merciless, piercing stare, catching a faint growl coming from under her breath. He resisted the urge to growl back.

-♠-

The late September sun felt good on Gary's face as he traversed the parched gravel road toward home, his school books slung over his shoulder in a leather strap. The trees, which lined both sides of the lane, were just beginning to turn from their summer's end green to varying shades of brown, orange and red, and birds chirped merrily in their branches. He kicked at a large rock. The events of the day replayed over and over in his mind, and as he thought of Ernie Spencer's bloodied face, he couldn't help but smile to himself. His knuckles still hurt, but he didn't care. It was all worth it.

"Hey, Gary! Gary Bell!" came a voice from behind.

Gary turned to see another kid trotting toward him. "Yeah?"

The boy finally caught up with him, panting slightly. "Frank Hawkins," he said, sticking out his hand to shake. He was about Gary's age, a bit taller, scrawny, with tousled brown hair and ears that stuck out like open car doors.

Gary reluctantly accepted the handshake. "Gary Bell..."

"Oh, I know who *you* are! The whole *school* knows now!"

"Huh?" His brow furrowed. "What do you mean?"

Frank took up his stride beside Gary. "That brawl you had with that sixth-grader today, Ernie whats-his-name. The whole school's talkin' about it!"

"Really?"

"Yup. I don't think you'll hafta worry about no one crossin' you again..."

"Hmm..." Gary resumed kicking the large rock as he walked, happy to hear this bit of information. "So... what do you want?"

Frank began kicking a stone of his own. "I heard what those other kids was sayin' about you... About your family and all."

"Yeah...?"

"Well, you see, I know how it feels. Kinda. My Pop got it in France. Got hit by a mortar shell, blown to smithereens..."

"Gosh... Sorry."

"Nah, it's alright. I don't remember too much about him anyway... He joined up in '42 when I was only three. But I know how hard it is dealin' with other kids who got Mas and Pas. Is still got my Ma, and my little Sis, but that's all, 'cept for aunts and uncles. You got any brothers or sisters?"

"Nope." Gary launched the rock into the field on their left.

"You got anybody?"

"Just my Gramps and Grandma. I live with them now, at least till my Pop comes home again..."

"Where'd he go?"

"Don't know."

Frank was silent for a moment. He adjusted his ball cap and asked, "Well... How long's he been gone?"

Gary cleared his throat and spit on the ground, not really wanting to talk about it. He sighed and said, "'Bout four years."

"Wow..."

"Where do you live?" Gary asked, just to change the subject.

"Over on Downing. Just past the old stone quarry. How 'bout you?"

"My Gramps' farm's up on Briggle Avenue. That's where I'm goin'."

"Well..." Frank thought for a moment. "My Ma's

workin' this evening. We own the bowling alley in town... You mind if I walk on with you?"

Gary hesitated. "Well... I got some chores to do..."

"I can help ya! We're pals now, you and me!"

Gary almost stopped walking. "We are?"

"Yep! And pals help their pals with chores." Frank slapped him on the back, smiling from ear to ear.

Gary wasn't sure if he liked the idea, but didn't know how to get out of the situation at this point. He wasn't really looking to be 'pals' with anyone. "Well... Okay, I guess..."

"Boy, your granny sure can cook, Gary..." Frank said, rubbing his belly as he lay back on the creek bank. "My Ma don't stand a chance against her..."

"Yeah, it's pretty good, I guess." Gary sat with his bare feet dangling in the gently running water. "I guess I'm just used to it. Pot roast ain't my favorite, though."

"Mine, neither, but that one was the best I ever ate. With my Ma gone most of the time, I usually just eat a cold sammich for supper. This was much better. Thanks for invitin' me over."

Gary didn't recall inviting him, but since he was slowly warming up to the idea of having someone around, and since Frank had helped him gather the eggs, he replied, "Sure thing, Frank."

"So what do you do for fun?"

"For fun? Hmm..." Gary thought for a moment. "I like playin' baseball and ridin' my bike... um, drivin' the tractor sometimes."

"You get to drive?"

"Sometimes. I like goin' for walks in the woods with my girl..."

Frank sat up. "You got a girl?"

"Yep." Frank didn't need to know that he'd only ever been in the woods with Maggie once, Gary thought, or that she wasn't technically 'his girl'. It still counted in his mind.

"What's her name? Who is she?"

"Margret Henchy. She lives right over the hill." Gary poked his thumb to the east.

"She pretty?"

"Yep. She's eleven."

"Wow... Have you ever... kissed her?"

Gary's mind wandered back to the awkward, yet amazing moment under the pear tree. "Oh, yeah, for sure. I've kissed lotsa girls." He figured the kissing booth at the fair the previous week counted, as well, where he'd spent two whole dollars on ten cent kisses, smooching multiple times with five different high school girls over the course of three days, until Grandma Kate cut off his cash flow, after finding out that he really hadn't been donating it to the church building fund after all. It slowly occurred to him that he'd had to pay for every kiss he'd ever received. That was something he needed to work on, otherwise he'd soon be completely penniless.

Frank leaned in closer, distractedly swatting at a fly that was buzzing about his head. "Really? What's it feel like to kiss a girl?"

Gary suddenly felt very grown up and wise. "Well, Frank, let me tell ya... It's just about the best thing ever, 'specially if she's pretty."

"Golly..." Frank slowly laid back down. "I never kissed a girl... 'cept my Momma, and that don't count for nothin'... I need to find a girl for my own."

"Well, there's plenty of them out there. You just gotta

go out and get 'em."

Frank sighed. "Yeah, I guess so... But where? Where do you find 'em?"

"Uhh..." Gary hadn't been prepared to back up his truth stretching. "All over the place... You going down to that dance thing this Friday night? That'd be a good place to find one."

"You mean that fundraiser for the Hoaglands? At the grange?"

"Yeah."

"I wasn't planning on going... Are you?"

"My Grandma's makin' pies for it, so I hafta go."

Frank sat up again, thinking for a moment. "And you think I could find a girl there?"

"Bound to be girls there, I'd say. Plus, then I wouldn't be stuck sellin' pies with my Grandma all night..."

"Well... if you promise to help me get one, I'll go."

Gary mulled this over in his mind. He really didn't have the slightest idea how to help Frank, but having someone else there besides his Grandma might be fun. Besides, how hard could it be?

"Okay?" Frank asked.

Gary turned toward him. "Sure, Frank. I'll find you a girl there." He cracked a smile, and added, "'cause pals find girls for their pals..."

"Alright, deal!" Frank exclaimed, grabbing Gary's hand and shaking it. "Boy, oh, boy... This is gonna be fun, ain't it, Gary?"

Gary took a deep breath and shifted his gaze to the sherbet colored sky. He wasn't sure how he was going to pull this one off... "Sure, pal. It'll be a gas...

Friday, September 23rd

Stars were beginning to speckle the navy blue sky as Gary made his way out of the grange hall and onto the brightly decorated patio, where dozens of couples were dancing the evening away to the bouncy, brassy sounds spewing from the live band of musicians in the corner, and dozens more men and women, all dressed in their Sunday best, milled about the edges of the large patio, sipping cocktails and smoking cigarettes. Light bulbs strung overhead cast them with a soft yellow glow. Gary breathed in the fresh air, glad to be relieved of his pie peddling duties inside the stuffy, crowded building, and searched the crowd for Frank, who was an hour late by his estimation. In the three days since their chat on the creek bank, Gary and Frank had become fast friends, and that whole time he'd silently been racking his brain about how to live up to his promise and snare Frank a dame. He had yet to come up with any sure fire, concrete ideas, although his grandpa had given him something worth trying...

As his eyes roamed over the throng, they settled on the glowing face of Candice Hauldman, a classmate of his, standing with a group of youngsters. She looked like an angel to him, dressed all in white, her long, curly blonde hair tied up with a small satin bow. Now *there* is a woman, he thought.

"Psst!" came a noise from the bushes to his left.

Gary swiveled around to find the source. "Frank?"

"Yeah, c'mere!" Frank whispered frantically, sticking his hand through the shrubs and motioning Gary over.

"What are you...?" Gary walked through a break in the bushes and found Frank standing next to his bicycle, wearing a dark suit and holding a pair of dripping wet shoes and socks in his hand. "What's...?"

Frank looked panicked. "I tried to take a short cut. I got stuck in a crick down the road a piece, and now my shoes are all wet and I don't know what to do!"

"What are you wearing?"

Frank glanced down at his clothes. "This is my funeral suit... Is it too much?"

"Uhh..."

"You look like a prisoner..." Frank said, pointing to Gary's black and white striped sweater and black pants.

Gary rolled his eyes. "I know. Don't remind me. My Grandma made me wear it. She was afraid I'd catch cold."

"What am I gonna do about my shoes?"

"Umm..." Gary thought for a moment. "Well, how wet are they?"

Frank tipped one of them upside down and several ounces of dirty creek water poured out. "Pretty wet..."

"Just put 'em back on. No one's gonna notice."

"You sure?"

"Yeah, what else are you gonna do? This ain't the beach. You're not gonna pick up any dames walkin' around barefoot."

"Well, okay..." Frank stooped down and pulled the sopping socks and shoes on. "You're the expert."

"Alright, now c'mere," Gary said, motioning to a gap in the bushes, the patchy light from the patio illuminating his face. "I've already got your first target."

"Really?" Frank came closer, peering through the shrubs. "Who?"

"Right there. In the white dress."

"Mrs. Durham?"

Gary leaned back, giving Frank an *'are you for real'* look. "Yeah, I want you to go pick up a thirty-year-old, married woman... No, dummy, the girl."

"Candice Hauldman? Gary, I don't think I can-"

"Listen. If you can nab Candy, you can get any girl

you want."

"But she's one of the most popular girls at school!"

"Exactly. Now here's what to do: I want you to go over there and start talking, but not to her."

"But, how-"

"Start talking to that other girl, the ugly one."

"Molly?"

"She's so ugly, I don't even know her name. It's Molly?"

"Yeah, Molly Todd."

"More like Molly 'Toad'..." Gary snorted. "Anyways, I want you to go over and start talking to her."

"How's that gonna help?"

"The idea is to make Candy jealous. Girls get jealous about stupid stuff. She's gonna wonder why you'd rather be talking to Dog Face Girl than with her, get it?"

"Ohhh... No, I don't get it. I shouldn't say anything to Candy?"

"Yeah, if she says something to you, you can answer, but you gotta act like you're not interested, got it?"

"Okay, and then what?"

"Then she should start trying to get *your* attention. After that, all you gotta do is tell her you wanna go someplace quiet, and then you kiss her. Easy as pie."

"I don't know, Gary... Where'd you learn all this? It sounds kinda shaky..."

"My Gramps. It's how he ended up marrying my Grandma. It works."

"Okay... If you say so."

Gary slapped him on the back. "Go on. You got nothin' to lose, right?"

"I guess not. Alright, here goes..."

A smile slowly spread across Gary's face as he

watched Frank approach the group of kids, leaving a trail of wet footprints on the concrete behind him. He pushed the branches aside to get a better view. Frank sauntered right up to Molly and began speaking to her, his back angled away from Candy. Perfect, Gary thought. If this actually worked, he was definitely going to try it. He secretly shared Frank's incredulity, but his Grandfather had insisted that he'd used this method to great effect in his early hound dog days.

Frank continued to speak with Molly, his gestures becoming more and more animated. He must have said something funny, because both of them laughed, which got Candy's attention. She leaned in on the conversation, smiling at Frank, who paid her absolutely no mind.

"Okay, Frankie," Gary whispered to himself, "don't overdo it..."

A few more minutes passed, with Frank and Molly laughing and Candy trying to join the conversation. At one point, she put her hand on Frank's shoulder and he moved away, completely turning his back on her.

"Too much, you dummy!" Gary hissed.

He watched dumbfounded as Frank took Molly by the arm and walked off of the patio and out into the orchard that surrounded the grange hall. He craned his neck to keep them in view, hoping that at any minute Frank would turn around and strike up a conversation with Candy, but he showed no signs of doing so. Gary leaned forward, resting all of his weight on one of the shrub branches. Bad idea. The branch snapped, sending his top half through the bushes and onto the patio with a thud. He frantically scrambled backward on his hands and knees, hoping that nobody had seen him, but when he looked back through the greenery, he saw someone approaching. Candice Hauldman. Damn.

"Gary Bell? Is that you?" She stooped down, peering

through the bushes.

"Uhh... H-hi, Candice..." Gary stood quickly, brushing himself off.

"What on Earth are you doing back there?"

"Oh, I was... just..." he stammered, "uh, just looking for someone..."

Candy walked around the group of shrubs, still looking puzzled. "Looking for someone?"

"Uh... *Thing*. Some*thing*."

"What?"

Gary searched his surroundings in dismay, frantically trying to think of something to find. His eyes fell on Frank's bicycle. "Uh, my friend's bike. That one." He pointed toward it.

"Oh, was it missing?"

"No, no... I just... wanted to make sure no one had stolen it..." He really needed to improve his quick thinking abilities, he thought.

"Oh... Who's your friend?"

"Frank Hawkins."

"Frank Hawkins? I was just trying to talk to him. He's really quite rude. Plus he smelled like he'd been playing in a pond..."

"Yeah," Gary laughed nervously, "that's Frank. Sometimes. But not always." He'd never actually been this close to Candy, and he felt his face beginning to heat up. She looked beautiful in the moonlight.

"I heard about your fight with Ernie Spencer the other day... That was pretty spectacular. I've actually been looking for you since I heard about it."

"Really?"

"Yes. He was such a bully. He was always pulling at my hair on the way home from school." She tugged at one of her long, curly locks. "So thank you."

"For what?"

"For putting him in his place." She took a step closer to him. "That was very brave of you..."

Gary's heart began beating faster than it already was. "Oh, w-well, you're welcome, then, Candice. I guess." He wiped the beading sweat off of his forehead.

"Oh, you can call me Candy. I guess you deserve a bravery reward..."

"A reward? Like w-what?"

Candice leaned in closer, closed her eyes and puckered her lips.

Gary's jaw hung open. He felt paralyzed. Candice was infinitely more beautiful than Maggie, not to mention she was one of, if not *the* most popular girl in fourth grade, and now she was offering him a kiss. Him, Gary Bell, who just a few days before was either one of two things: a complete unknown or a whipping boy, definitely not someone that Candice Hauldman would ever even consider speaking to, much less lock lips with.

"Well?" she prompted, opening one eye and re-puckering.

Gary squeezed his eyes shut and leaned into her kiss, all the while trying to convince himself that this wasn't a dream. Her lips were warm and soft, and she smelled of vanilla. In that instant, he ranked those three seconds as the best three seconds of his life. Nothing else even came close. Candy pulled away.

"There," she said, smiling. "There's your reward."

"Uhh... Th-thank you..." It was all he could do to speak.

"Maybe you could walk me home from school from now on?"

"Y-yeah, yes... sure, good... I can do that. If you'd like..."

"I would like you to."

"Okay..." Gary couldn't believe that any of this was

actually happening. He hadn't even planned on trying to find a girl tonight, and now he was going to get to walk the prettiest one he knew home from school every day. Now he was glad Frank had blown it.

"Okay, well... I have to get back before my parents start to wonder where I am... See you at school?"

"Yeah, of course. I'll be there."

"Alright," she said, leaning over and kissing him on the cheek. "Bye, Gary..."

"Yeah, see you later... Candy..."

"Wow..." Frank said, his grin stretching his freshly kissed lips to new limits. "That was amazing."

"I can't believe you kissed that thing," Gary said, disgusted. They walked slowly along the deserted gravel road, Frank pushing his bicycle, his shoes still squishing with every footfall. In the passing hours, the air had cooled considerably; their breath came out in puffy clouds, catching the moonlight, making Gary thankful that his Grandmother had forced him to wear the sweater. He ran his hand through the fox tails that grew alongside the lane.

"And I can't believe you kissed Candice Hauldman... You're gonna be a regular legend around these parts, Gary Bell," Frank said, laughing.

"I can't believe it either... How come you went and kissed that other one?"

Frank looked up to the star-spattered sky. "I don't know, really... I just started talkin' to her and she seemed like a really nice girl. I think most people prolly don't even give her a chance 'cause she ain't that pretty."

"She sure ain't..."

"Hey," Frank laughed again, "careful. That's my girl you're talkin' about!"

Gary smiled. "Is that what you call it?"

"Alright, alright... So she ain't gonna be in Esquire any time soon."

"*Esquire?* She ain't even gonna be in the Farm and Dairy!"

"Yeah," Frank said, still grinning, "but I don't care..."

"Well, that's all that matters, I guess."

"Darn tootin'!" Frank slowed to a stop as they came to Downing Street. "Here's my stop, pal."

"Alright... See you tomorrow?"

"You bet." Frank began to walk away, and then added, "Oh, and one more thing..." He stopped and turned around.

"Yeah?"

"Now that we both got girls, we need to promise we'll never let 'em come between us, okay? We gotta remember to always be pals first, ladykillers second."

Gary snorted in amusement, gazing out across the rolling, moonlit hills. "Sure thing, Frankie. Pals first." He looked back toward his new, best and only friend and nodded slowly. "And pals forever..."

Chapter 3
Whitefeather

Friday, July 14th, 1950 - Age 11

"But, Gramps..." Gary said, smacking his suitcase against his leg, "do I really hafta stay here?" His eyes roamed over the crowd of fifty or so boys all milling about beneath a large, road straddling plank sign that read 'Camp Whitefeather' in carved letters. The camp, as far as he could see, was heavily wooded and situated on a gentle incline, with cabins, shanties and pavilions staggered about the hillside, all peeking through the thick, green vegetation. Dirt paths linked everything together. A deep frown began pulling at his face as he watched the young campers all bidding farewell to their parents.

"Of course you have to stay, Gary," Roy said. He shut the car door and handed Gary a denim jacket. "You'll have fun. Why, I used to spend every summer up here when I was your age."

"But there ain't even any girls here, Gramps... And look how many kids are here. There's too many."

Roy rustled Gary's hair. "It'll be good for you, boy. Make some friends. You need to learn how to get along with all folks, anyway, not just girls."

Gary sighed. He didn't need to learn that, because he didn't ever plan on needing the knowledge. "But I already got Frank for my friend. One's enough for me." He kicked at the gravel and then began scanning the crowd. "Where is he, anyway? If he don't show up, can I come home?"

"This is not a debate, Gary. I'll be back to get you in two weeks." He slapped Gary on the back. "Whether you enjoy yourself until then is entirely up to you."

Gary grunted. There was no way possible he was going to enjoy himself. No girls, no bicycles, no privacy... just a bunch of stupid, stinky boys that were all going to try and steal the Hershey bar that he'd hidden in his suitcase.

Roy glanced at his wristwatch. "I promised your grandmother I'd take her to Cibo's tonight, so I need to get along. Goodbye, Gary," he said, getting back into his car and starting it. "Try to keep yourself out of trouble."

Gary managed a half-hearted wave, with the mention of his favorite Italian restaurant only making the matter worse. He watched, in disgust, as his grandfather's sedan bounced away down the winding gravel road, disappearing through the dense trees. For a moment, he imagined himself running off into the woods and hiding out for the next two weeks, but then realized he would have needed to bring a lot more candy bars. And perhaps some toilet paper. Stupid camp, he thought, slapping at a mosquito as he turned back to face the mob of boys that were being corralled into a large, log-style meeting hall. What a waste of two perfectly good weeks.

He was just about to give in and join the group when he heard a car barreling up the drive. A moment later, a black Ford came around the bend and ground to a halt in front of Gary, raising a cloud of dust that made him cough. It was Frank, with his mother at the helm.

"Gary!" Frank said, shoving his door open.

"You made it..."

"Yep! Mom ran over a turtle on the way here." He jumped out of the car. "That's why I'm late."

"You were supposed to be here at five. I was startin' to think you weren't gonna show up."

"Naw, I wouldn't miss this for the world!"

Gary watched as Mrs. Hawkins walked back to the trunk and opened it for Frank. "Hello, Gary," she said, smiling.

"Hi, Mrs. Hawkins..." Gary said quietly. Lily Ann Hawkins was the most dazzling creature that he had ever laid eyes on, even more so than Candy, and she looked especially alluring today, with her breezy, floral print sundress, cherry red lipstick and long, dark eyelashes. For her to have been a high fashion model or some famous actress took no stretch of Gary's imagination. He had no idea how floppy-eared Frank could've come out of her perfect body, and secretly assumed that the only explanation was that Frank was adopted. In addition to her tall, slender, textbook beauty, she always seemed to be so carefree and perhaps just a little bit too reckless, which was attractive to Gary, and made him wish he'd been born a few years earlier. 'A few years' being about twenty. She was also the only woman that he'd ever seen completely naked. He'd hidden himself in the cattails one night while she was swimming in her pond, Bathsheba style. But every time he recalled spying on Lily in all of her jay bird glory, moonlight glistening off of her slick, porcelain skin, a feeling of deep guilt jabbed him in the stomach like a hot poker. He quickly halted his thoughts.

"Are you going to keep my Frankie out of trouble?" Lily asked, helping Frank pull a massive suitcase from the trunk.

"Aww," Frank said, grunting against the weight of his luggage, "c'mon, Ma..."

"Sure, Mrs. Hawkins. I plan on gettin' out for good behavior, anyways."

"Oh, what's the matter?" she asked. "Don't you enjoy summer camp?"

"Yeah," Frank said, "what's wrong with you? You communist or somethin'?"

"I don't know, Mrs. H... I never been to camp before. Somehow I always managed to get out of coming here. But I don't think I'm gonna like it..."

"Aww, darling," she said, pushing her lower lip out slightly, "You boys are going to have a wonderful time." She leaned down until her bright green eyes were even with his. As she spoke, her breath came out smelling of sweet peaches. She gently lifted his chin up with her white cotton clad fingers, and added, "I promise."

She had no idea what she was doing to him, Gary thought. Either she had taken pity on him for the fact that he had no mother, and was trying to make him feel extra special, or she had a hankering for eleven-year-old boys. And as much as he hoped against it, he figured it was probably the former scenario. "Okay..." he replied.

"Frank always has a marvelous time here," she said, standing up straight.

"Yep. Every year." Frank quickly began dragging his suitcase toward the meeting hall, calling over his shoulder,

"And with you here, Gary, it's gonna be a real gas! C'mon, let's go!"

Lily put her arm around Gary's shoulder and squeezed him in a half-hug. "You going to be alright?"

"Yeah, I'll be fine. Thanks, Mrs. Hawkins. So long." He grabbed his suitcase by the handle and pulled away from her.

"Bye, Gary," she said, and then yelled, waving, "Bye, Frankie! Behave!"

"Bye, Momma!"

"What in the world do you have in that thing?" Gary asked, eyeing Frank's enormous suitcase sitting next to his. They were settling in to their small, rough-hewn cabin, along with eight other Mohawks, which was the group they'd been assigned to, having survived the long and, to Gary, mind-numbing first camp meeting, where he learned that his duties would include peeling potatoes, fetching water, disposing of trash and getting along with his fellow camp mates. It was pretty much how he envisioned prison.

"I got all kinds of stuff in here," Frank said, dragging the old leather case up unto the bottom bunk and unzipping it. "Clothes, first-aid kit, toothbrush and paste... and this." He pulled out a small, portable radio and held it up, caressing its semi-translucent red plastic casing. "So we can listen to the Indians."

"Good idea."

"Other than that, it's just normal campin' stuff. Like matches and calamine goop."

Gary wiped the sweat from his forehead as he looked

around the lantern-illuminated cabin. The five bunk beds that lined the walls took up most of the space, leaving just enough room in the center for a small wooden table and several chairs. One of the other Mohawks, a chunky youngster with curly dark hair, squeezed his way through the group of boys toward Gary. He stuck his hand out to shake.

"Hi! I'm Eddie Vinsen! You're Gary Bell!"

This was exactly what he'd been trying to avoid since he'd arrived. He reluctantly returned the handshake. "Hi."

"Your girl is Candice Hauldman! You were in the fifth grade, right?"

"Yep."

"You're the guy that beat up that other guy! I'm gonna be in the third grade this year. I can't wait!"

"That's great," Gary said, turning back toward Frank, trying to brush the kid off, pegging him as the first suspect if his Hershey bar went missing. But Eddie persisted.

"You live in Carson Creek don't you? With your grand-"

"Yeah." Gary slid his suitcase under the bed. "Frank, can I have the bottom bunk?" It was going to be hot enough close to the floor, let alone trying to sleep next to the ceiling.

"Oh... gosh, Gary..." Frank said, sounding reluctant. "I kinda... Tell ya what..." He reached into his pocket and pulled out a nickel. "I'll flip you for it."

"That's what I did!" Eddie chimed in. "But I lost..."

"I guess a fifty-fifty shot is better'n nothin'..." Gary said to Frank, still trying to ignore the new kid, and silently thanking God that he wasn't the one who had to sleep under Fat Eddie's bunk.

"Heads or tails?" Frank got the coin into position.

"Buffalo."

The nickel sang as Frank flicked it high into the air,

bouncing it off the ceiling. It clattered to the floorboards at Eddie's feet.

"What is it?" Gary asked.

"Sorry, pal! It's a Indian!" Eddie laughed. "Looks like you get to-"

"Fine," Gary cut him off. "I really actually wanted the top bunk anyways..." he lied, climbing up to his perch. He was going to bed before the night got any worse.

"Sorry, Gary," Frank said, pulling his shirt off.

"No big deal." Gary had to hunch low in order not to hit his head on the ceiling as he removed his jeans. "You won fair and square. 'Night."

"What? You're not goin' to sleep already are you?"

"Yeah, why not?"

"Well, after lights out, we always stay up and tell ghost stories. I've been savin' up some good ones."

Gary rubbed his eyes and feigned a yawn. "I'm whooped. Maybe tomorrow night."

"You're such a party pooper, Gary, you know that?"

"Yep. Goodnight, Frankie..."

Sleep was nowhere to be found. Without a clock or watch, Gary guessed it to be about three or four o'clock in the morning, maybe later, and he had yet to grab a single wink. Sweat rolled off of his face and onto the concrete sack that the organizers of Camp Whitefeather surely had mistaken for a pillow. Beneath him, Frank's bed-rattling snores sounded like a freight train with a sick engine. Freight Train Frankie. That was a good nickname, Gary thought. He wondered what his nickname could be, and if it would be acceptable to assign it to himself instead of waiting for someone less creative to give him one. It should be something tough and maybe a little ominous, not something funny. Gary the Grave Digger? Maybe that was a bit much. This was going to require some serious thought, he realized.

As he continued to ponder monikers, he slowly became aware of thunder rumbling off in the distance. It started out just a low, pulsing growl in the sky, but soon turned to hair-raising peals that cracked like falling timber, accompanied by strobes of cabin-illuminating lightning. Then the rain began to fall. Hard. It sounded like truckloads of marbles were being dropped onto the corrugated steel roof, just above Gary's head.

"Oh, wonderful..." he muttered quietly.

Just after daybreak, rain still falling steadily, the sun fully obscured by the dark, cloudy sky, the cabin door swung open and their counselor, Mr. Danny Royce, stomped in. Danny, decked out in a rain poncho and tall rubber boots, was seventeen, the high school track champion, and had been coming to Camp Whitefeather since he was five years old. Gary had learned the night before that his preferred nickname was 'Zeus', due to the lightning bolt-shaped shock of white that ran through the side of his otherwise black hair, which is what had kicked off Gary's thoughts about nicknames in the first place. Zeus seemed like a nice enough guy to him, and he liked his nickname.

"Alright, fellas!" Zeus bellowed, pulling back his poncho hood, "Up and at 'em!"

The boys seemed split on wanting to get up, with a

few moaning, and the rest hopping out of their beds enthusiastically. Gary reluctantly sat up.

"Let's go, we got a big day ahead of us! Rise and shine, Mr. Hawkins!"

Gary leaned over the bunk to see Frank still fast asleep, his snoring amplified by his wide open mouth. Zeus walked over and kicked the bunk. Frank slowly snorted his way out of dreamland and opened his eyes.

"Where am I?" he asked, confused, rubbing the sandmen away.

Zeus didn't answer, instead he turned to address the rest of the Mohawks. "Okay, fellas. We're gonna hit the showers and then head on over to the mess hall for breakfast. After that, hopefully this pesky rain will go away and we can get started with our activities. Grab your gear and let's head out, okay?"

Gary sighed and slid off of the bunk. Maybe it would rain all day and camp would be canceled.

Try as he might, Gary couldn't complain about breakfast; fluffy scrambled eggs, juicy sausage links and perfectly crisp bacon all went down his gullet with ease, followed by deliciously creamy ice cold milk. Grandma Kate always had a tendency to over-cook her eggs, and bacon was mostly reserved for Sunday mornings, so both came as a welcome surprise. But he reminded himself not to enjoy it too much; he was bound and determined to stay upset about this whole ordeal being forced upon him. He took another sip of milk and scanned the noisy mess hall. Another group of boys had burst into some sort of fake Indian tribal song, slamming their fists on the table and beating their chests. A few of them let out war cries.

"What in the world are they doing?" he asked Frank, who was sitting next to him, shoveling eggs into his mouth like it was the last meal he'd ever eat.

"Camp songs," he managed to say with his mouth full. After he swallowed, he elaborated, "Every group has their own songs that they sing all the time. You'd better get used to it, 'cause it ain't gonna stop 'till we go home."

"That's stupid. I ain't singin' nothin'."

"Aww, c'mon... It's fun. You'll see. My favorite song of ours, of the Mohawks, is *'Spookum'.*"

"Huh?"

"It goes like this..." Frank cleared his throat and began to sing in a rhythmic tribal tone:

> *"Ooh la Layla*
> *A riki tiki rhumba*
> *Spooky spookum spooky spook*
> *Miss a baby Mohawk*

> *"Ooh la Lola*
> *Icky drippy tick tock*
> *Spooky spookum spooky spook*
> *Bloody footprints on the dock..."*

By this time, the whole group had begun to sing along, including Zeus, who was pounding out an Indian-style beat on the rough wooden table. Their voices grew louder as they reached the final verse:

> *"Ooh la Lila*
> *Ooey gooey splish splosh*
> *Spooky spookum spooky spook*
> *Comin' for you chop chop!"*

With the last line, they all made slashing motions across their necks and finished the song by yelling, "Ooo spookum!" followed by whoops and cheers.

"See?" Frank said, settling back into his spot on the bench, all smiles, "It's fun!"

Slightly stunned, Gary sat his milk down on the table without a word.

"It's about Princess Whitefeather! Zeus wrote it a long time ago and now we sing it every year."

"But Whitefeather wasn't a Mohawk. She was Iroquois."

"Not the way Zeus tells the story. He's got the best version I've ever heard! I'll make sure he tells it at the campfire tonight."

Gary turned to look out the window. "I don't think we're gonna be having any campfires if this rain don't let up. Which'd be fine by me... Maybe we'd get to go home early."

"Aww, c'mon, Gary, snap out of it! Quit bein' such a stick in the mud."

Gary didn't reply. He wanted to be a stick in the mud. And Frank's incessant happiness was only strengthening his resolve. There were a hundred things he'd rather be doing; out hunting groundhogs with Huey, or fishing in Henchy's pond, or necking in the woods with Candy. Heck, he'd rather be at home doing chores. Anything would be better than being forced to stay here with all these dumb boys.

The snap and crackle of the campfire, married with the low whine of crickets, frogs, cicadas and all other manner of woodland nightlife, served as background music for the various tales of ghosts, ghouls, murderers, werewolves, evil school teachers and anything else the small group of campers could come up with. Smoke from the fire had mingled with a heavy fog to blanket the small clearing, which was situated between the woods on one side, and a swift-moving stream on the the other. Gary, not at all swayed in his viewpoint of camp after his first full day, of which two-thirds had consisted of rain, and the other third of drying out their cabin, sat on a fallen tree next to Frank, a raincoat serving as a barrier between his blue jeans and the still-wet log. He stared directly into the fire, only half listening to Eddie Vinson's jumbled account of an escaped ax murderer who had, over the course of the story, curiously gone from only killing his parents, to killing an entire camp full of kids. Of course, he still roamed these very same woods, hunting for more unwitting children to chop up. What a bunch of baloney, Gary thought.

Finally, Eddie's tale was brought to an end and the group was silent for a moment. Gary aimlessly poked a stick into the mud at his feet, waiting for the next poorly-crafted, so-called 'scary' story to begin. All he could think about was that he was missing Sid Caesar on television. His grandparents had only bought the set a month ago, and already he was being forced to skip his favorite program.

"Hey, Zeus?" Frank piped up beside him. "How 'bout tellin' us your Princess Whitefeather story? Gary here hasn't ever heard it."

"Well, now," Zeus said, leaning forward on his log, "that's not a half-bad idea, Frankie... Whatcha say, Gary?"

Zeus was one of the bright spots at camp, Gary conceded, if not the only bright spot. He'd done his very best to keep them all entertained during the long, dreary day, and, with his Jerry Lewis impression, had even made

Gary laugh, which didn't happen often, especially not when he had already set his mood dial to 'sour'. He'd only heard snippets of Whitefeather's story before, so he nodded and said, "Okay."

"Alright, swell..." Zeus cleared his throat and lowered his voice a bit. "But I'll warn you fellas, it's not a good idea to tell it next to running water... You sure you still wanna hear it?"

The circle nodded an emphatic 'yes'.

"Okay, here goes... It all began way back before any of us were born. Before your grandfathers and your grandfather's grandfathers were born. Whitefeather, named for the eagle feather she wore in her hair, was the most beautiful Indian princess that had ever walked the Earth, and she had fallen in love with a young scout from an enemy tribe named Lone Wolf. She didn't dare tell her father, Chief Long Arrow of the Mohawks, lest he hunt down and kill Lone Wolf. The Chief was very, very protective of Whitefeather since her mother had died, and would not stand having her in the arms of the enemy, so she kept it a secret. For months, she would sneak away into the woods and meet Lone Wolf and speak of their predicament.

"Finally, one day, unable to bear the weight of passion any longer, Lone Wolf told the princess that he wanted her to be his bride. He said that they could escape and start a new tribe somewhere, far, far away from there. Whitefeather agreed and they set a date to journey off, but not before they had joined themselves together in holy matrimony.

"As the day for their escape drew near, Whitefeather became anxious. She began acting strangely around her father, and he knew that something was wrong. Ever suspicious, he decided to look through his daughter's belongings, where he found Whitefeather's most precious possessions packed in a small satchel, but even more condemning, he found a love letter to her from Lone Wolf, one that she hadn't been able to bring herself to burn. In a rage, Long Arrow locked the princess away in a cave, far up on a cliff side. There she stayed for many days and nights, many, many weeks, all the while hoping that Lone Wolf would come to her rescue, but he never came.

"Now, as time passed, Whitefeather began to realize that she was going to have a baby. And, fearing what would become of the child if her father found out, she decided to escape herself. She sharpened a piece of stone into a long knife and waited for her caretaker to arrive with her supper. When he came and opened the gate to the cave, Whitefeather pounced on him and killed him, slitting his throat. Now even more scared, and covered in the blood of her own tribesman, the princess ran to find Lone Wolf. She called for him and called for him, but he did not answer her.

"But her cries were heard by a Mohawk scout, who found her and chased her deeper into the woods, trying to capture her and take her back to her father. She escaped him, but now she was lost beyond all hope. She laid down next to a stream and cried herself to sleep.

"She was awakened in the morning by someone kneeling next to her. She jumped up and pulled out her knife, ready to defend her life, but then she realized it was Lone Wolf, cut and whipped and bleeding. She was overjoyed to see him, but asked him what had happened. He told her that he had waited for her for months, coming each day to their spot in the woods, but when she never arrived, he became more and more worried and went to look for her. But he was captured by Long Arrow and had been punished unmercifully; tied between two trees and beaten and whipped until he passed out from the pain. He was then thrown into a cage until Long Arrow could think up a fitting enough death for him.

"But the night before, a scout had returned and announced that Princess Whitefeather had escaped her prison and killed her caretaker. Having heard this, Chief Long Arrow erupted in a rage and gathered the entire tribe together into a search party to find her. With no one left to guard his cage, Lone Wolf escaped and had followed her trail to the stream.

"Whitefeather and Lone Wolf then took off into the forest, heading west, determined to leave behind all of the calamity that had beset them. They traveled for days, covered many miles, but along the way, Long Arrow and his men, unrelenting in their resolve to recapture the princess and Lone Wolf, had picked up their trail, and were closing in fast. To make matters worse, as they crossed over mountains and forded streams, Whitefeather had become weary, and it was obvious that she was about to give birth, which she did. It was a boy, and Lone Wolf and Whitefeather were so happy with their little family. But it didn't last long.

"One night, while they were sleeping, Long Arrow and his men ambushed them, finally having caught up. Lone Wolf leaped up and began to fight off the entire tribe singlehandedly with his spear. He yelled for Whitefeather to escape with their son, and said that he would catch up with her, but even then she knew that she had seen the last of her beloved Lone Wolf. He stood his ground with great valor and bravery, but her father's men were too many, and fell upon him with their arrows, knives and tomahawks like wolves on a wounded deer, tearing him apart piece by piece.

"With tears of sadness streaming down her face, she ran off into the woods, but not before a stray arrow zipped past her newborn son, cutting his tender skin. Tears of sadness turned to tears of rage as she ran with all of her strength. Miles passed, days passed, and soon it was obvious that her baby boy was very sick. Though she had tended to his wound, the cut from the arrow had grown infected; it had been a poison arrow.

"Finally, she came to a lake, and, confident that she had lost her father and his men, built a small shelter out of branches and leaves where she tried to nurse her baby back to health. But it was not to be. The boy died a few days later and, weeping deeply, she fashioned together a small raft and drifted out and buried him on a island in the middle of the lake.

"As she was kneeling at her son's grave, she spotted them; a large group of Indians on the shore across from her, headed by her father, Long Arrow. He called to her, saying that it was time for her to give up, come back home, put all of this behind them. But the sight of her father only enraged Whitefeather. She thought of her brave and beloved Lone Wolf, and now her lost child. She had no home to return to. Her home had already passed into the afterlife.

"With her father and his entire tribe looking on, Princess Whitefeather, in all of her sad beauty, stood up and walked into the lake and disappeared beneath its surface. When she didn't resurface, the men began to look for her underwater, swimming out to the spot where she had gone under, but she was nowhere to be found. All that was left was a brilliant white eagle's feather floating on the surface of the lake.

"Years passed, and the legend grew that Whitefeather's spirit lives in the waters of the lake, and in its streams, and in any bit of running water nearby. They say that she still haunts the area, seeking revenge for the deaths of her loved ones. Sometimes she reappears in human form, but now as a decayed, rotting corpse; the physical evidence of her inner torment. Over the centuries, she has become blinded by her ever growing rage, and will now unmercifully kill anyone in her path, wielding that same stone knife that she had chiseled out in her cell so long ago, slicing men's throats and then dragging them back into the lake with her. They say that no one is safe, and that a dripping faucet is a telltale sign that her spirit is coming for you, one drop of water at a time."

In the dying orange glow of the campfire, the entire group sat completely silent and wide-eyed, including Gary. He had never heard this bit of local folklore before in such detail, and knew that he would never forget it after hearing Zeus' perfectly narrated account.

"And that," Zeus said, "is the story of Princess Whitefeather."

"Is that all true?" one of the boys asked.

"You want me to call up Whitefeather's spirit so you can find out?" Zeus replied.

"No!" several in the group shouted.

"Okay, then."

Frank leaned over toward Gary. "See? I told you so."

Gary nodded, visibly impressed. He couldn't wait to ask Grandpa Roy if he knew about all this.

Zeus looked at his watch. "Okay, fellas, I think it's time we turned in for the night. Who wants to lead the way back to camp?" When no one raised their hand, he chuckled. "Alright, alright. I'll lead the way. But just remember that you guys asked for it, so if you can't sleep tonight, don't come whining to me..."

Indeed, Gary couldn't sleep, but it wasn't on account of him being scared or afraid. He couldn't stop thinking about Zeus' story. He was pretty sure that the whole animated corpse part was added on just to scare kids, and that Zeus may have embellished a bit, or maybe even made up the whole thing, but for some reason several parts of the tale had resonated with him. Especially the character of Lone Wolf, who was obviously the most important piece of the puzzle, in his mind at least. He tried to imagine being so brave, and wondered if he would ever love someone enough to willingly die for them in such an awful manner. It was the same way he felt whenever he saw paintings of Jesus on the cross, and his grandma would always say, 'See, Gary? He did that for you and me...'. He couldn't think of anyone he'd die for, and it made him somewhat sad. Grandpa Roy always told him that if you have something to die for, then you have something to live for. Why was he even living?

The other thing that had begun to take shape in his mind centered around his nickname. 'Lone Wolf' was definitely in the running. It seemed to sum up everything he wished he could be and everything he was, all at once. Plus it sounded tough.

"Psst... Gary?" Frank's whisper floated up from the bottom bunk. "You awake?"

Frank was probably scared witless, Gary thought, and almost didn't answer him because it served him right for being such a baby and buying into those spooky stories. But he decided he'd take the high road and whispered back, "Yeah, what?"

"I gotta go to the bathroom. You wanna walk down to the outhouse with me?"

Gary sighed. "Why? You scared?"

"No... we're not s'posed to go out after dark by ourselves."

Sighing again, louder this time, Gary pushed off the bed sheets. "Alright..."

As they crossed through the deserted camp, it was apparent that the fog had redoubled its efforts to completely obscure everything from view. The few lights that were sporadically placed throughout the compound were nothing more than soft yellow orbs peeking through the trees, their usually bright glow stifled by the haze. Gary thought the whole place looked like something out of a science fiction movie. Even the flashlight that Frank was wielding only served to illuminate about three feet in front of them, and it was three feet worth of fog and nothing else. They finally located the wooden steps that led up to the next tier of the camp and began to ascend them.

"Maybe if you hadn't eaten all those marshmallows we wouldn't be coming out here..." Gary said.

"Do you think that story about Whitefeather is true?" Frank asked.

"No. At least not all of it. Not the part about her coming back from the dead, anyway."

"But what if it is? I mean, how could you know?"

"Frank. Please. That type of stuff is just made up to scare scarebabies. You ain't a scarebaby, are ya?"

"Well... no... I don't think so."

"People don't just come back from the dead."

"What about Jesus?"

"*Jesus?* C'mon, Frankie. Whitefeather wasn't God. And Jesus didn't come back to cut people up an' drag 'em into some lake." They reached the top of the stairs and headed for the outhouses.

"I guess not..."

"You guess not?"

"I mean, no, you're right."

"Darn straight I'm right. Quit bein' a scaredy cat. It ain't manly."

"Okay..." Frank said as they reached the outhouses, which, like everything else in the camp, were brown-stained, rough-hewn log buildings nestled among clusters of pine trees. A small light hung on the wall beside the door.

"I'll wait for you out here," Gary said, leaning up against the building.

"I'll just be a minute. Maybe two," Frank called over his shoulder as he pushed open the swinging door.

"Take your time, pal..." Gary looked around to make sure no one else was in sight and then pulled a half-spent cigarette from his shirt pocket, along with the Zippo he'd purchased with his birthday money. He chuckled softly as he lit up, remembering how he'd convinced his grandmother that he was buying the lighter as a gift for Grandpa Roy, so she wouldn't be able to tell him about it. Though, to be honest, he was pretty sure Gramps knew he was smoking. It was only a matter of time before the dreaded 'we need to talk' talk. As he was taking a long drag, his thoughts were interrupted by the sound of a twig snapping in the distance, coming from his right. He froze. For a split second, all of the horribly told ghost stories he'd been subjected to earlier that night flooded back into his memory, sending a shiver down his spine. He tried to peer into the darkness, but the fog was far too thick. Whatever it was, it was coming down the hill through the woods behind the camp office, which was only about thirty feet away from where he stood.

"H-hello?" he called.

"What?" Frank replied from inside the outhouse.

"Shhh!" Gary hushed.

The sound stopped for a moment, waited, and then changed direction. It was now heading straight for him. Gary tensed and the hair on the back of his neck stood up, but he forced himself to take his own advice and not be a scaredy cat. Or at least to not show it. It was probably just Zeus or one of the other camp counselors.

"Who's there?" he asked, trying to keep his voice even. "Zeus?" A moment later, shrouded in the fog, a man came into view. Tall, burly and carrying a satchel over one shoulder, he was walking with a pronounced limp. It wasn't Zeus. As he came further into the light, Gary could see that he was absolutely filthy; his pants and shoes were completely caked with mud, as was his once-white, collared shirt. A loosened tie hung about his neck. Equally grimy was his dirt-streaked, thirty-something face, which was twisted into a decided scowl the likes of which Gary had never seen. The uneasy feeling in his stomach that he'd been trying to hold at bay began to flood over the dam.

"Who're you?" the man asked, sounding hoarse. "What're you doing out here?"

"Uhh..." Gary stuttered, "I'm Gary Bell..." He immediately realized that giving out his full name to a person like this probably hadn't been a very wise thing to do. Up close, he noticed that the man was sweating profusely, and his clothes were not only filthy, they were torn and tattered. Gary would have instantly assumed he was a bum were it not for his alligator shoes and obviously expensive wristwatch. "Who are you?"

"Mind your own goddamn business, kid." He coughed and spit a wad of phlegm out. "Which way's the road?"

Gary decided he didn't like this guy one bit. He pegged him as some sort of gangster or some such type, and he wasn't about to help him. "Uhh... I don't know, let me get a counselor to-" Before he could finish his sentence, the man grabbed him by the collar and slammed him against the outhouse wall, pinning him there.

"I wouldn't advise that," he hissed. "You'll keep your goddamn trap shut if you know what's good for you, boy..."

Gary's head had smacked into the wall hard enough that he was seeing stars. Whatever this thug was wrapped up in must be some serious business, he thought. "O-okay..." he managed.

"Okay. Now... which way was the road?"

"Over that way." Gary pointed. "Past the big cabin." It was no longer about helping the guy, it was about getting him out of there as quickly as possible.

"That's better," he growled, letting go of Gary's shirt. "Alright, Gary Bell. You never saw me or anyone else out here tonight, you got that?"

Gary nodded slowly.

"'Cause if I find out you said otherwise..." He jabbed his finger in Gary's chest. "I'm gonna come lookin' for you. And I don't play nice."

"O-okay..."

Just as quickly as he had appeared, the man vanished into the haze, heading toward the camp exit. Gary was dumbfounded. He let out a deep breath he'd been holding in and tried to make sense of the whole ordeal, and as he did, his anger began to grow hotter. The outhouse door slowly opened.

"What in tarnation was that all about?" Frank asked quietly.

"I wish I knew," Gary said, rubbing the back of his head. The man had tapped deep into his temper vein, and, dangerous or not, he wasn't going to stand for it. "But I'd sure like to find out..."

The next day was packed to the gills with activities, due to the previous day's rainout; hiking, canoeing, archery, dodgeball, a vicious game of capture the flag, and, to top it all off, a swim in the camp pond, all of which had escaped Gary's full concentration, and the last of which he refused to participate in altogether. The events of the night before kept running through his mind. Something big or important was going on over the hill and he hated not knowing what it was, especially after gaining a rather large bump on the head because of it. Illuminated by flecks of setting sun dancing off of the pond, he sat at the edge with his feet dangling in the water, trying to formulate a plan. By then, only a handful of boys remained in the water, the rest having retreated to the cabin.

"What's up, buddy?" a voice came from behind.

Gary, slightly startled, turned to see Zeus walking towards him, still wearing his swim trunks, drying his hair with a large towel. "Oh, hey, Zeus. Not much."

"Don't you like swimming?" he asked, sitting down next to Gary.

"It's alright."

"Or..." he paused, "maybe it's just camp in general that you're not all that excited about."

Gary thought for a moment. "Did Frank tell you that?"

"No, no... it's been pretty obvious."

"Oh. Sorry."

"No, it's alright. You know, I first came here in '39, when I was seven?"

"Really?"

"Yup. And I felt the exact same way then that you do now."

"Really? You didn't like it?"

"Hated it. It was the first time I'd been away from my parents, I didn't know anybody... I felt like I'd been shipped off to prison or something."

Gary smiled to himself; that was his sentiment exactly. "So why'd you come back then, if you hated it?"

"Well... I think after the first week I just kinda got used to it. And then I started to like it, made friends, etcetera, etcetera."

"Hmm... I'm not sure if I'll get used to it."

"I never thought I would've, either. But now, after all these years..." Zeus turned his eyes from Gary to their surroundings. He seemed to be soaking in everything; sights, sounds and smells; the tall pines swaying in the light breeze, birds merrily singing, the smell of the woodland earth. "Now, this place is like a second home to me. It's gonna be rough saying goodbye..."

"'Goodbye'? Won't they let you come back?"

"Oh, I'm sure they would. But I'm probably not gonna be able to come back, not for a few years, anyway."

"How come?"

"Well," Zeus sighed, "I'm leaving for the Marines at the end of the month... Then I'm getting shipped off to Korea, most likely."

"Gosh..." Gary exclaimed quietly.

"Yup. That's what I'm starting to think. Gonna be tough..."

A weighty silence descended between them. As the water lapped at his feet, Gary once again questioned his own bravery and fortitude, now in light of Zeus'.

"But," Zeus finally spoke again, in a sober tone, "somebody's gotta do it. If everyone always ran away from everything that scared them, where would we be? I mean, what if George Washington hadn't crossed the Delaware and fought against the British?" It sounded more like he was trying to strengthen his own resolve than ask a question.

"You're prob'ly right."

"You gotta face your fears, stand up to what scares

you, even if it's tough. Even if it's the toughest thing you've ever done..." Then, suddenly, as if snapping out of a trance, his smile returned and he slapped Gary on the back. "And you never know; even something as bad as summer camp could turn out to be fun."

Gary smiled back and nodded. "Maybe." He snatched up a rock and threw it into the pond. "But how's come you're spendin' your last two weeks here with us? Shouldn't you be with your family?"

"I am with my family, buddy. You guys are like family."

"But you hardly even know me."

"True. But I'll bet by the end of the next two weeks I'll know you a whole lot better. I think it's important that I spend this time doing something worthwhile, you know? Something that'll leave a lasting impression."

"Yeah... I think I get you."

"So make my life a little easier and at least pretend to have a good time, okay?" he laughed. "At least make me think I'm doing something good for you."

Gary smiled again. "Okay, I'll try..."

"Okay, good. I gotta go check up on the other guys. You coming along?"

"Nah, I think I'm gonna stay here 'till Frankie's done swimming," Gary replied, pointing across the pond toward Frank, who was trying, and failing, to do an underwater handstand.

"Alright. Don't let him drown."

"I'll try not to. No promises."

After Zeus had gone, Gary, lost in thought, continued to skip stones across the pond until one of them veered off and hit Frank in the arm.

"Hey!" Frank yelled from across the water. "What gives?"

Gary, though he hadn't intended to get Frank's

attention, motioned him over.

Frank said something to the other three boys who were still swimming and then waded over to Gary. "What?" he asked, rubbing his eyes.

"We need to talk. I think I'm gonna go for a little walk tonight." Zeus' little speech about not running from what scared him was all he needed to make up his mind.

Frank turned to make sure the other boys were out of earshot and then, in a lowered voice, said, "Are you sure that's a good idea? I mean, shouldn't we tell someone?"

"No." Gary shook his head. "They'd just try an' stop us."

"'Us'?"

"What, you're not gonna turn chicken on me, are ya?"

"No, it's just that I planned on surviving summer camp. That guy seemed pretty serious."

"Yeah..." Gary said, rubbing the bump on the back of his head. "But I figure if we're careful and go after dark, we should be okay. Somethin' important is goin' on up there. Maybe somethin' really big."

"Maybe, but what if he catches us? How will you even know where to go or look?"

"Like I said, we'll just hafta be careful. Now look, I was wearin' this shirt last night," he said, tugging at his collar. "Look at these marks."

"What about 'em?"

Gary pointed to the black fingerprints the man had left behind when he had grabbed him and thrown him into the outhouse wall. "This ain't dirt, see?" He rubbed some of the residue off on his fingers and showed Frank. "You know what that is?"

"What?"

"That's coal, Frankie, plain as day. Now when he was a kid, my Gramps worked in a coal mine somewhere up there, and I'll bet you dollars to doughnuts that that's where that guy came from. I remember he had black smudges on his face, too."

Frank raised his eyebrows. "Hmm... That'd be a good hideout, for sure. But how would you find it?"

"It can't be that hard to find. That guy was bound to leave some sorta trail or footprints or somethin'. We know where he came outta the woods. We'll just hafta start there."

"I still don't know, Gary... If no one knows where we are and then that fella catches us..." He rubbed his neck nervously. "Well, I don't think it'd end up too good for us."

"You gotta stop thinkin' the worst case of everything. What if there's a bunch'a money up there or somethin'? Think of it that way. I can tell you this, whatever's up there, that guy seemed to think it was important. And what a hood like that thinks is important is always either money, or worth money."

"I guess you could be right... but..." Frank wrinkled his nose and shook his head. "I still don't think it's smart."

Gary sighed, exasperated. "Look, Frank... How about this: we go up there, find the mine, and then wait an' see if that guy shows up. We'll hide somewhere so he don't see us. Then if he goes inside, we'll come back and get the police. Where's the danger in that? I just... that fella made me mad and I just wanna know what he's up to."

"Well..." Frank said slowly, "We wouldn't go near the mine? I mean, we wouldn't go inside? 'Cause I seen in movies where-"

"No. We'd just hide outside somewhere and wait to see if he shows up. How 'bout it?"

"And we'll come straight back and tell someone?"

"We'll come directly back an' call the coppers down on him. Deal?"

Frank took a deep breath. "I just don't-"

"Frankie, Jesus *Criminy!*" Gary exclaimed, flopping

onto his back. "Fine. I'll go by myself."

"No, no... I guess... Alright. Let's do it."

Gary sat up quickly, and before Frank could change his mind, he said, "We leave at midnight."

"Okay, you got your flashlight?" Gary asked in a whisper.

"Yeah, right here." Frank held up the light and switched it on.

"No, no!" Gary hissed, covering the lamp with his hand. "Shut it off! Someone'll see it!"

They stood between the camp office and the outhouses, in the exact spot the mysterious man had emerged from the woods the previous evening. The night air was warm and thick with humidity, as well as with mosquitoes, which swarmed all about them in little, vicious, bloodsucking clouds. Gary smacked at one and whispered, "Alright. Let's go."

The man's trail was easy enough to trace; he'd obviously not been worried about leaving the hillside unspoiled. Trampled foliage, broken branches and large footprints in the moist earth littered their path, which seemed to take them in a zig-zag pattern, even in circles at times. It was clearly apparent that the man had been lost.

"Somebody needs to buy this fella a compass for Christmas..." Frank said.

"Tell me about it. If he wasn't lost, he was drunk as a boiled owl." Gary thought for a moment. "You know, last night he said that 'I hadn't seen him or anyone else'... There must be more than just him."

"Great. Now you tell me this?"

"I just thought of it. He must've gotten separated from the other one, or ones, and that's why he was walking around in circles."

"Makes sense, I guess..." Frank coughed. "Gary, I ain't gonna try and pull any wool over your eyes; I'm kinda not... not scared."

"Oh, we'll be fine. Quit worryin'..." Gary thought this might be the appropriate time to pass along some of Zeus' wisdom, in the form of his own, of course. "Let me tell ya, Frankie, I've learned that you can't always run away from what scares you. You gotta stand up to-"

"Shh!" Frank hushed.

"What?"

"Did you hear that?"

"Hear what?" Gary whispered.

"Behind us..."

They were now close to a half mile away from the edge of camp, and turned to look back through the trees. A branch snapped somewhere down the hill, not far away. Gary, his heart rate instantly picking up, shoved Frank off of the path and into the thick undergrowth, where they crouched down and waited, trying to silence their heavy breathing.

"Maybe it's just a deer..." Gary said as quietly as possible.

"Or maybe it's just a ax murderer..." Frank replied. "I told you this was a bad-"

"Shh!"

The sound steadily drew closer. Who or whatever it was wasn't trying to be stealthy, so maybe it hadn't heard them and they would be safe, Gary hoped. He listened as branches snapped, leaves rustled and brush swished, and then came a rather loud sound that seemed entirely out of place and was definitely unexpected.

"Was that a... a *fart?*" Frank whispered, eyes wide,

half-smiling through his fear.

Gary had to cover his mouth to keep from laughing, but he wasn't entirely successful.

"Shh!" Frank said.

"No, you *'shh'!*" Gary hushed back, his voice broken by poorly stifled laughter.

"Hello?" Came a voice from the path. "Guys?"

Gary shot up from his crouched position to see a short, rotund silhouette standing just a few feet away. "What the-? *Eddie?* What the sam hill are you doin' up here?"

Frank stood up, as well, and flipped on the flashlight. "Eddie?"

Eddie Vinson, dressed only in his pajamas, squinted at the beam. "Hey, guys," he said, waving his pudgy hand somewhat sheepishly. "Excuse me..."

"Holy Moses..." Gary sighed in relief. "What are you doing here?"

"I saw you guys leave the camp. Where are you goin'?"

"We're goin' to find-" Frank started, but was cut off by Gary's glare.

"You have to go back," Gary said. "You can't come with us." The last thing they needed was a snotty-nosed butterball tagging along behind them, alerting the entire forest of their presence.

"But..." Eddie's expression fell.

"No. We're doin' somethin' important. We need to have our full concentration." Gary lowered his voice. "And we really need to be quiet."

"Somethin' important? What?" A serious look crossed over his ruddy face. "Are you guys lookin' for Whitefeather's ghost?"

"What? No... It's a secret. Can't tell you."

"Aww, c'mon."

"No. *N.O.* You have to go back down to camp now. It's... it's not safe up here."

"Not safe?" Eddie asked, puzzled. "Does Zeus know you're up here? 'Cause we ain't supposed to leave camp..."

Gary growled softly to himself.

"C'mon. I wanna come, too. If you let me come I'll keep it a secret. I'll be quiet as a church mouse. I promise."

"Gary," Frank said, "let's just go back. We can't-"

"No. We're not going back. *I'm* not going back." He stepped out of the bushes and back onto the path. "You can if you want, but I'm not."

"Then we'll have to take him along. If we don't, he'll tell Zeus where we are."

Gary sighed. "This is a bad idea, Frank. Fine... But he's your responsibility. If he gets killed up here, I'm not tellin' his parents."

"Killed?" Eddie chirped.

"Look, Eddie," Gary said, his annoyance completely apparent, "stay right behind us, keep your mouth shut and don't do anything stupid."

"Mm'kay... Like what?"

"Anything. Just don't do anything." Gary began tracing the path again, leading the way. "Pretend like you're not here."

"But how do I-"

"Just... be quiet. Okay?"

"Mm'kay, I'll try..."

Over the next twenty minutes, it became apparent that while Eddie may have been trying to be quiet, it wasn't in his nature to succeed. Gary thought it would've been better if they had been dragging a china cabinet along behind them; it would have been an improvement over Eddie's huffing, puffing, thrashing, grunting and stumbling. And, as their luck would have it, Eddie also seemed to be severely allergic to everything he touched. He couldn't stop sneezing.

"Good grief..." Gary said softly. "It's a wonder the whole county doesn't know we're here..."

"Sorry," Eddie offered. "It's my allergies. I have allergies."

"Well, stop havin' allergies. I told you we gotta be quiet. You're gonna blow the whole thing. Pinch your nose shut or something."

Eddie tried this for a while, but it just made him cough. "Snot's runnin' down my throat," he complained.

Gary stopped and turned around, moved Frank aside and poked his finger in Eddie's chest. "Look here, you little... I didn't ask you to come along. I didn't *want* you to come along. If you don't shut up, I'm gonna give you a good shove and let you roll back to camp. You got it?"

Eddie nodded quickly. "Mm'kay. Got it."

"Good. No more coughing. No more sneezing. No more anything or you're gettin' a one-way ticket shaped like my boot."

Finally, after an hour of trudging, walking in circles and waiting for Eddie to catch up, they reached the top of the ridge. Whitefeather Lake spread out below them like a black mirror, its southern shore coming to rest about three hundred yards down the heavily wooded hill, which was considerably steeper on this side, and its opposing shore barely visible ten miles to the north. The gently rippling water shimmered in the moonlight. Gary put his hands on his hips, surveying the landscape.

"Now what?" Frank asked.

Something caught Gary's eye. "Look!" He pointed down the hill to their left where, about a football field away, what appeared to be headlights were bouncing through the woods, heading east.

"Is that a car?"

Gary began descending the hill. "Looks like it. C'mon, let's go find out..."

They tried to keep up with the vehicle as best as they could, cutting across the incline as quickly and quietly as possible. Gary's heartbeat had begun racing again. He felt like a big game hunter or a soldier running toward his prey. He couldn't help but wish that he had his revolver with him, but, unfortunately, he hadn't had the room in his suitcase to bring it to camp. If something went wrong, he'd have to think fast.

"Wait, look," he said, "they're stopping..."

They snuck to within a stone's throw of what turned out to be an old, muddy pickup truck sitting below them on an overgrown, out of service logging road. Gary crouched behind a fallen tree and motioned for Frank and Eddie to get down beside him. A door slammed. Peering over the log, Gary watched as two men got out of the truck, one of them was carrying a lantern and the other man, who Gary instantly recognized as his assailant from the night before, was brandishing a shotgun.

"Criminy, that's a big gun," Frank whispered.

"Yeah..."

"Who are they?" Eddie asked.

"Shhh."

They watched as the men, both well dressed, wearing fedoras and smoking cigarettes, walked to a pile of branches on the hillside and began pulling them away, eventually revealing an opening about four feet across and six feet high, framed in with old, weather cracked boards.

"The mine!" Gary exclaimed quietly. "See? I told

you!"

The lantern was lit, and the two men disappeared inside.

"Okay," Frank said, slowly backing away, "you saw 'em go in. Now we go back and call the police."

"No, wait," Gary began to protest.

"No, you promised. This is gettin' dangerous. He's got a shotgun, Gary. Let's go."

Gary looked back toward the mine and thought for a moment. "You go. I'll wait here 'till you get back."

"Gary, that wasn't the plan. What happens if-"

"Just hurry up and go. Leave me the flashlight."

"What? No, Gary! C'mon!"

"I'm stayin' right here, Frank. I'm gonna keep an eye on 'em. Go get the cops."

"Why do you want the flashlight?"

"Just in case... In case I need to signal you or somethin'. I'll use morse code."

"I don't know morse code," Frank said.

"Neither do I, but we'll figure it out. Now hurry up!"

Frank shook his head slowly. "I don't like this, Gary."

"I don't care. Someone needs to stay here."

"Fine... stay right here. I'll be back as fast as I can."

"Take him with you," Gary said, pointing to Eddie. "Hurry."

"Okay..." Frank began to retreat up the hill, and then turned back. "Gary?"

"Yeah?"

"Don't do anything stupid."

"Who, me? Go on, get outta here."

Gary watched as Frank and Eddie disappeared into the woods and then turned back toward the mine. He desperately wanted to know what was going on in there, but even he, as reckless as he was at times, especially when someone had gotten under his skin, wasn't foolish enough to try and find out. He figured a shotgun wound was an exception to the rule of not running away from things that scared him.

Time passed slowly. He kept his eyes glued to the entrance, watching for any sign of movement or activity. At one point, he heard some angry, muffled voices coming from inside, but was too far away to make out any actual words. Come on, Frank, he thought. Two consecutive nights of very little rest were beginning to catch up with him, and he was worried that if he sat there too much longer he'd fall asleep. Then he saw it: a faint glow dancing off of the walls of the mineshaft. Before long, it spilled outside onto the ground, followed quickly by its source, the lantern, which was being held high by one of the men.

"You comin'?" Gary heard him ask.

The second man emerged. "Yeah. When are we supposed to meet this guy?" Gary felt his anger begin to rise again at the sight of the man who'd roughed him up.

"Half hour. Then we meet the others at the cemetery. Then, after we come back here and get our stuff, we're gone for good, brother."

After re-covering the entrance with branches, they got into the truck and disappeared down the logging road.

Damn it, Gary thought. He had hoped that Frank would show up with the cops before the men left. Now they would have to wait for them to return for their 'stuff', as the man had said. "Hmm... What kinda 'stuff'?" he wondered out loud as he stood up, stretching. Surely it couldn't hurt to have a little peek...

Throwing the branches aside, he cautiously stepped into the mineshaft, switching on Frank's flashlight to illuminate his way. The air was musty and damp, almost sticky, and the dirt floor was littered with fresh footprints, which he began to follow. In the pitch darkness, even with the light, he could only see a short distance in front of him, and an uneasy, claustrophobic feeling began to settle on his shoulders. He shuddered it off and kept going. No running away, he reminded himself.

After going about fifty feet into the mine, the footprints took a right turn into an offshoot of the main shaft. He stopped to listen, making sure that he was truly alone. When he heard nothing, he swung the flashlight beam to the right and stepped through the log-braced opening.

It seemed to be more like a long, narrow storage room rather than another shaft. Directly in front of the entryway stood a small wooden table with three mismatched chairs surrounding it. On top sat what looked like a woman's purse and an empty ashtray, but, more importantly, a shotgun. He froze. After a moment, he remembered that the man hadn't taken it with him in the truck. He let out a sigh of relief, laughing nervously to himself.

Then the sound of something slowly scraping across the floor emerged from the darkness to his left.

Every hair on his body stood up. He began to tremble. Had it just been his imagination? Or maybe an echo? Slowly, against his will and better judgment, he turned the light in the direction of the sound, keeping it angled toward the floor so he could just get a peek. He hoped against hope that it had been nothing, but he got ready to run, just in case. The beam circle crawled across the dirt, rocks and cigarette butts that covered the ground. A shoe came into the light. Followed by a dirty pair of *human feet.*

Gary dropped the flashlight and fell backward out of

the room, his heart immediately racing and his breath coming deep and fast. He quickly shuffled backward until he ran into the main shaft's opposing wall. He wasn't alone after all.

"Mmmm..." came a muffled groan from inside the room. "Hhhmmm..."

He tried to hold his breath and listen. Whoever it was wasn't coming out to get him, he realized. Carefully weighing his options, he decided against bolting for the mine's exit. Fear was squeezing his stomach like a boa constrictor, and his sense of self preservation was trying to drag him back outside to safety, but a deeper, more uncanny feeling that he couldn't name was compelling him to stay and investigate.

"Hhmmmmrrr..."

He gulped and sat up on his knees. He had to face his fear. Wiping the sweat out of his eyes, he slowly crawled back into the room and reached for the flashlight.

"Mmmm..." the groan came again, followed by what sounded like a whimper.

He stood up and, with more than a little trepidation, turned the light back toward the corner. What came into view was not at all what he had expected. The body of a young woman, scantily clad in nothing but torn, black underwear, had been lashed to a chair with heavy rope and was laying on her side in the dirt. What Gary could only guess had once been her dress was wrapped around her head.

"H-hello?" he croaked.

"Mmm... *Mmm!*" Her feet kicked as much as the ropes would allow.

She must be gagged, he thought. Stepping closer, he could see that her bare legs were covered in scratches and caked with dirt. If her figure was any indication, Gary pegged her to be in her late teens or early twenties. He bent down and gently put his hand on her leg. She stopped kicking. Sitting the flashlight on the ground, he reached up and, with shaking hands, began removing the torn dress from around her head, slowly. As it fell away, her face came into view; she was a brunette, with dark, bloodshot brown eyes that squinted at the light. Even in her present state, Gary thought she was gorgeous. The dress had kept her face relatively clean and, save for the streaked mascara that had run down her cheeks, even her makeup was in place. She looked like belonged in Hollywood. He set to work untying the gag. The knot was tight, but eventually broke free and the young woman gasped for fresh air.

"It's alright, it's alright," he tried to comfort her. "Who are you? What's your name?"

She began to cry, but managed to speak through her tears. "Charlotte... My name is Charlotte. Please. Please untie me..."

"Right, of course," Gary replied quickly, looking for the ends of the ropes.

"Can you... sit me up? My arm is stuck under the chair..."

Kicking the flashlight out of the way, Gary stood up and grabbed the chair and, with a bit of struggle and grunting, lifted it back onto its feet. He pulled out his pocket knife and made short work of the rope around her wrists.

"Thank you..."

"What's going on here, Charlotte?" Gary asked, beginning to saw through the rest of her bindings.

"Those men..." She coughed and began trying to rub life back into her hands. "Those men kidnapped me."

"But why?" The rope broke loose and Gary began to unwind it.

"For money... My father is Rodney Emmling."

"What?" Gary stopped for a moment. "Mayor

Emmling? From Catalpa?"

"Yes... They grabbed me three nights ago. At least I think it's been that long..."

"You've been in here that whole time?"

Charlotte began to weep even deeper, her shoulders heaving as the ropes finally fell free. "Yes... How did you find me?"

"I... I don't know. I knew something was going on up here, but I had no idea... Can you walk okay? Are you hurt bad?"

"No, I think I can walk..." She tried to stand, but her legs buckled, not having been used for the better part of seventy-two hours.

"Here," Gary said, putting his arm around her, "hang on to me. We gotta get you outta here..." If it had been under any other circumstances, he would probably have fainted at his luck; holding on to a barely clothed, beautiful young woman like Charlotte wasn't something he got to do everyday. She was quite a bit taller than him though, which made it difficult to help her walk.

"Ouch!" she exclaimed, stumbling slightly.

"Just... lean on me. I gotcha."

"Thank you..." She sniffled.

The sound of a slamming car door echoed down the mine shaft from outside. They stopped in their tracks.

"Oh, no!" Charlotte gasped.

Maybe it was Frank with the police, Gary thought. Then he heard a somewhat familiar voice.

"...can't believe you forgot the shotgun... Hey... didn't we cover this up...?"

"Shit!" Gary hissed. Now was the time for quick thinking. "Uhh, c'mon, get back in the corner!" He grabbed Charlotte and half shoved, half dragged her into the darkness, and then grabbed the flashlight and switched it off. The shotgun. He felt his way to the table and snatched it up, and then retreated to the corner, pressing his back up against Charlotte, staying between her and the door.

The sound of heavy footsteps began echoing through the mine. "...think she got loose?" he heard one of the men ask.

"Better not have... Cause if she did and I catch her, she's gonna get it a lot worse than last time... I'll kill her. I don't care... Give me the lantern..."

They were trapped. Gary could feel Charlotte's heart beating rapidly, pounding against his back, beating almost as fast as his own. He felt for her hand. "Here," he whispered, passing her the flashlight. "As soon as you see him, turn that on, right in his face."

"O-okay..."

He positioned the shotgun, pointing it toward the door. He wasn't sure if he had it in him to kill a man if need be, but he was about to find out.

The lantern swung into the room. Charlotte immediately switched on the flashlight. Gary hoped that it would obscure the man's vision enough to keep him from realizing that he was about to have a showdown with an eleven year old kid.

"Well, well, well..." the man said. "How'd you get loose, pumpkin?"

"Stay back!" Gary yelled, trying to make his voice sound a little deeper. "I got your gun!"

The man, the same man from the night before, squinted into the light. "Who're you, kid?" He took a step closer.

"I said, I got your gun! Get the hell outta here!"

The man held the lantern a little closer and then a look of realization spread across his face. He snickered wickedly. "Well, if it isn't the little camping twerp..."

"What's going on in here, Joe?" The second man

entered the room.

"Oh, just a wee bit of comedy relief here, Marty. We're being held up by this little boy blue."

"Oh, really... Come on, kid. Give us the gun. Give it up, little boy blue." They both laughed.

Gary's blood began to boil. Keep pushing, he thought.

"Nah," the man named Joe said, "he doesn't need to give me the gun. It isn't even loaded."

Gary stopped breathing for a moment. How could it not be loaded? Could his luck really be that bad? He saw Joe's eyes dance from him to the barrel of the gun and back. Was he bluffing? "Alright, then... Come take it from me."

Joe's face clouded over. "Listen here, you little bastard. You're gonna bring me that shotgun because I said so, not because I can't come get it. I'm the one in charge here..."

"Not 'till you prove it, you're not," Gary said, cocking both barrels with a loud 'clunk'. If, in fact, the gun wasn't loaded, he thought maybe he could get close enough to use it as a club. He took a step forward, pulling Charlotte behind him.

"Kid, I'm warning you. This is not going to end well for you if you don't cut the bullshit. Give me the gun."

"Get outta my way..." Gary growled, taking another step. "Get back." He thought he may have seen Joe flinch slightly.

"Jesus, Marty," he said, rubbing his eyes, " kids these days..." He looked back at Gary. "Okay, listen, boy. Here's how this is going to work. I'm going to give you a chance to get out of here with your guts where they belong. You hand over the shotgun, and you can go. Simple as that. I promise you, you will never get a better offer than that from me."

Gary stopped advancing. "What about Charlotte?" he asked.

"I said, you can go. We need her. Besides, she's not going to get hurt, not unless you don't do what I tell you. Not unless you do something stupid."

He thought briefly. He wanted nothing more than to get out of there and as far away as he possibly could. This whole ordeal had gone much worse than he had ever anticipated. But he also knew, deep down, that he couldn't leave Charlotte to these hoods. Who knows what they'd do to her now. He made his decision. "No. She goes with me. And I'm leaving right now."

"Okay, kid. Have it your way. Don't say I didn't offer. What do you say, Marty?"

Gary scarcely had time to mentally process Joe and Marty's lightning fast movements. Joe bowled into him with his full weight, knocking he and Charlotte over, sending the flashlight sailing into the wall, breaking its bulb. The lantern, which had still been in Joe's hand, followed suit. They were instantly thrown into pitch darkness. Joe and Marty both landed on top of him, with Marty wrapping his hands around Gary's neck and Joe grabbing the barrels of the shotgun, trying to yank it out of Gary's hands. It was the last mistake he'd ever make. With Gary's index finger still wrapped around the triggers, the violent tugging set the gun off, illuminating the room for one, brilliant, deafening split second, in which he saw the left side of Joe's face disappear, and all of Marty's. It sounded like a cannon had gone off in his hands. An instant later, the room went dark again, and he felt the men collapse on top of him, felt himself being drenched with a warm, thick liquid. Blood. "Ch-Charlotte? Are you okay?" he asked, barely able to hear himself over the ringing in his ears.

"Oh my God... Oh my *God*..."

"What? *What?* Are you hurt?" He grunted as he writhed out from beneath the lifeless forms of Joe and Marty. He began feeling around in the dark for Charlotte. "Where are you?"

"Oh my God... What just happened? What happened...?"

Gary's hand found her arm and he tried his best to lift her up. "They're gone. Are you hurt?"

"No... No I'm okay I think... Where's the light?"

"We gotta get you outta here. You don't wanna be able to see right now, trust me. C'mon."

"What happened?"

"I... They... Let's get the hell outta here..."

To Gary, stumbling out of the mine and into the fresh night air felt like being reborn. He took in a deep breath as he helped Charlotte to the ground. Both of them were still trembling with adrenaline.

"Oh my God!" Charlotte exclaimed, seeing Gary in the moonlight. "You're bleeding!"

Gary looked himself over. He was covered from his head to his waist in blood, soaked completely. "No... I don't think it's mine..." he said, trying to wipe it from his eyes. He spit some out on the ground.

"Are you sure?"

"Pretty sure..." He collapsed next to her.

"Okay... If you say so." She was still speaking through a steady stream of tears, but they were slowly turning into tears of joy. "What's your name?"

"Gary. Gary Bell."

"How old are you?"

"Eleven."

"Well, Gary Bell... all I can say is thank you. Thank you for rescuing me." She put her arms around him and gave him a weak hug.

Gary managed a smile. "Anytime..." Something up on the hill caught his attention. He turned to see a group of flashlight beams bobbing wildly, coming towards them in haste. If it was more bad guys and not Frank with the police, he decided he was giving up immediately.

"Gary!" Frank yelled.

"Frank!" Gary replied, jumping up, having never been happier to see his friend. Frank was followed by Zeus and four police officers.

"Are you okay? We heard a gunshot!" Frank said, bursting out of the undergrowth. "Holy Moses! What happened? Are you okay? Are you bleeding?"

"I'm fine, I'm fine..."

One of the officers caught up with Frank. "Gary? I'm Officer Bowman... You're *sure* you're okay, son?"

Gary nodded and stepped aside to reveal Charlotte. "But I think she needs some help."

"Who's this?" Bowman asked, surprised.

"Charlotte Emmling. The Mayor's daughter. They kidnapped her."

A look of incredulity spread across Bowman's face. He swung around and barked some orders to one of the other policemen, who ran off, and he then turned back to Gary. "Where are they? Did they get away?"

"No... I don't think they're goin' anywhere... They're in there," he said, pointing to the mineshaft, "first door on the right."

As Bowman and another officer went to inspect the mine, Zeus, shaking his head, stepped up. "Gary... you're supposed to get in trouble for this sort of thing, but..." He glanced at Charlotte. "I guess we can make an exception this time. You're a regular Lone Wolf!" he laughed, slapping Gary on the back. "Only you lived through the whole thing! I'm proud of you, buddy."

Gary smiled. He was proud, too; he'd proved something to himself, about himself. He realized that bravery wasn't about not being afraid or scared, it was about being afraid and scared and not letting it stop him. He felt like he'd grown up, like he'd discovered something about himself that he had no idea existed, and it was a wonderful feeling. Standing there, exhausted, soaked in blood and still trembling, he had never had a clearer picture of what it meant to be a man. He looked back at Charlotte. He wanted to thank her for being his Whitefeather, for giving him something to fight for, but he knew she wouldn't understand. He simply smiled at her.

He had a feeling that the realization of all that had transpired that night would eventually come crashing down on him. He felt like crying, but he'd save that for later. "Yeah, that's me, I guess..." he said, taking another deep breath and turning back to Frank and Zeus, offering them a weary grin, "Gary 'The Lone Wolf' Bell..."

Friday, July 28th - 13 days later

"All set?" Frank asked as he pulled his enormous suitcase off of his bed, letting it slam to the floor.

"Yeah, I guess..." Gary replied, looking around the cabin. Although it hadn't done much to change his introverted ways, the last two weeks had been life-altering beyond anything he could have ever imagined, and, as much as he hated to admit it to himself, he was going to miss being there.

The days just after the mineshaft incident had been full of police questionings, news reporter interviews and even a dinner with the Mayor of Catalpa, who had expressed his gratitude with, among other things, a $500 savings bond. He'd even gotten a kiss from Charlotte; on the cheek, of course. But the whole ordeal had left him exhausted, and being there in the days that followed had allowed him time to recuperate somewhat. Twice, he'd returned to the mine before it had been sealed off by the police. As he'd walked back into its dark, musty confines, he'd been able to come to grips with what had happened there and what he'd been forced to do, though it was still hard for him to believe that it hadn't all been a dream. While he had been there, he'd even picked up a souvenir from the dirty floor, which he now pulled from his jeans' pocket. It was an old, weathered ace of spades card, bent and faded and flecked with the blood of his assailants. Zeus had said it was called the 'death card', which Gary found amusing, seeing as how he'd had to kill two men to get it. It was his new good luck charm. Sliding it back into his pocket, he reached down and picked up his luggage, and then turned to Frank. "Yeah... I'm ready."

Chapter 4
The Long Way Home

Friday, April 13th, 1951 - Age 12

    Gary knew something was wrong. As he walked up the driveway, schoolbooks slung over his shoulder, he could see both of his grandparents waiting for him on the front porch, standing with their arms crossed. They didn't look happy. His mind immediately shot to all of the things he'd done that they might have found out about; stealing cigarettes, swiping whiskey, sneaking out at night to meet Candy, throwing firecrackers in the hen house... it could be a myriad of things that he'd rather keep secret. As he got closer, he could make out tears glistening in Kate's eyes. Great, he thought. It must be really bad. Maybe they discovered the girly pictures he'd stashed in the hay loft. He'd have to come up with a scapegoat pretty fast if that were the case. He slowly approached the front steps.

"Gary..." Kate began, her voice wavering, "we have some bad news, darling..."

"Bad news?" He asked, secretly relieved that it wasn't the old *'We need to talk young man'* line that he'd heard so many times.

"Yes... It's..." She brought a handkerchief to her nose and fresh tears welled up in her eyes.. "You tell him, Roy."

Grandpa Roy crouched down. "Gary, I'm afraid it's about Huey..."

Gary felt the blood drain from his face. His heart began pounding. "W-what? What about him?"

"He's... he's no longer with us."

"What...?" he asked, confused, trying to hold back his emotions. "What happened?"

"Well... he... he got hit."

Gary failed to keep his tear ducts closed. "Like, by a car?"

"Yes." Roy reached out and pulled him into his arms. Kate followed suit.

"I'm so sorry, sweetie," she said.

He couldn't believe it. "No... no, not Huey..." he said, burying his face in Roy's coat.

"Do you want to say goodbye?" Roy asked. "He's in the barn."

Gary pulled away and nodded slowly, wiping his nose on his jacket sleeve.

"Okay. Let me know when you're done and I'll... lay him to rest."

"No," Gary said, "I'll do it. I'll bury him..."

He slowly rolled the barn door back on its creaky wheels, afraid to look inside. He only had two real friends in the whole world, Huey and Frank, and he couldn't believe that now he was down to one. Why did life have to be so fragile? What was the point of it all? He wished he could just die and get it over with, and never again have to deal with the death of a loved one. It was too painful.

He forced himself to look into the barn. Huey was laying on a canvas tarp in the middle of the straw-littered floor, his fur dark and matted with dirt and blood; one of his hind legs was twisted at an odd angle. An eerie stillness hung in the air. Gary reluctantly stepped inside the aged building and slowly shuffled toward his fallen comrade, his eyelids brimming with a new wave of sadness. He got down on his knees.

"Hey, boy..." he sniffled, running his hand across the pup's dirty coat. He noticed a bullet hole at the base of the skull; apparently Gramps had been forced to finish the job. "I'm so sorry..." He removed the leather collar from around Huey's neck, stuffed it in his jacket pocket, and, trying not to imagine the last few moments of his life, undoubtedly full of terrible yelps and screeching tires, took one final look at his friend and then gently began folding the canvas around him. He stood and found a short piece of rope and laced it through the eyelets bordering the tarp, tied it tight, and then fetched a shovel from the wall. Turning back toward Huey he said softly, "Alright, boy. Let's go for one last walk."

Following the trail along the creek and up through the field, a path he and Huey had taken hundreds of times, a flood of memories broke into his mind. He recalled the first day he'd met the pup, on his fifth birthday as a gift from his mother. He was just a runt then, with sad brown eyes, a bright tan coat and a constantly wagging tail. His mother had reasoned that Gary should have at least one friend, someone to play with and talk to, someone to care for, and since he didn't want to be around any other children, a puppy was the next best thing. She had been right. Until he had met Frank, Huey was his only confidant, sticking by his side through thick and thin, always there to bring a smile or lap away tears, always ready to listen to his musings. He was the best sidekick a boy could ask for. He remembered hunting rabbits, sled riding, swimming, playing fetch, sharing stolen cookies, and, when it got cold and he was permitted to stay in the house, being able to wake up in the middle of the night and hear Huey's soft snoring at the foot of the bed. They were treasured memories, ones that he would never forget. And over time, Huey's eyesight had begun to dim, gray fur slowly crept into his coat and he wasn't able to run and jump and play as he had when he was younger, but his tail never stopped wagging. Somehow Gary knew that the deep feelings of love, friendship and trust were all mutual, and that Huey was just as appreciative of Gary as Gary was of him.

As he approached the tree line at the top of the field, he readjusted his grip on the tarp and squeezed between the naked blackberry bushes. Huey was getting heavy. The rope had begun to dig into his shoulder and he was forced to switch sides. "Almost there, boy," he said, planting the shovel in the ground. Careful not to drop the canvas, he transferred it from one shoulder to the other, and then continued on up the hill.

Save for a few crows cawing off in the distance, the small clearing was completely still and quiet, like a sanctuary. The grass had yet to return to its vibrant green after enduring the long, cold winter, and dead leaves still littered its patchy brown surface. The poor old pear tree stood off to the right, looking as sad as ever. Gary assumed that it was gone for good and that its only service to the world now would be to hide his treasures in its hollow. He removed the tarp from his shoulder, gently placed it on the ground, and sunk the shovel into the earth.

It took him close to an hour before he was satisfied with Huey's final resting place, having dug four feet down, passing through still-frozen ground and a nearly impenetrable spider's web of tree roots. The light had begun to fade from the sky overhead, taking with it a handful of degrees off of the already low thermometer, but Gary had worked up a considerable sweat, and had long since removed his heavy jacket. Steam rolled off of his back in swirling plumes as he threw the shovel out of the hole and reached for Huey. This was the end of the line. He pulled the canvas across the grass and down into the hole, cradling it in his arms. As hard as he tried, more tears could not be held back. He spoke with a wavering voice. "Goodbye, pal. You were the best friend I've ever had. Prob'ly the best friend I'll ever have in my whole entire life, and I'll never replace you. I couldn't even if I wanted to." He slowly lowered Huey to the bottom, carefully, as if he were lowering a baby into a cradle. Patting the tarp one last time, he added, "I love you, Huey. I won't ever forget you..."

Grandma Kate was waiting for him on the back porch, illuminated by a light on the wall. "Are you okay, dear?" she asked as he neared.

No, he wasn't okay in the slightest sense of the word.

He'd drug his feet the whole way back to the house, not ready to accept a world without his best pal. He wished he could start all over again, back to when he was five and Huey was just a puppy. All of the hardships along the way would be worth reliving if he could overcome them with Huey at his side. Now all he had was Frank. "Yeah, I'm okay, Grandma," he lied.

"Are you hungry? I made your favorite: spaghetti and meatballs."

Gary decided that he needed to start being more truthful, as spaghetti and meatballs were definitely not his favorite. He'd rather have a cheeseburger any night of the week. Except tonight. Tonight he'd rather eat poisonous mushrooms. "Thanks, Grandma, but I'm not really hungry."

Kate looked worried. "Are you sure, dear? I know you're sad, but you mustn't go without your supper. I even made an apple pie for dessert."

Gary wasn't listening. He was focused on a tuft of Huey's fur that was stuck to the corner of one of the wooden porch steps. He needed to get away from there. "Is it alright if I call Frank and see if I can spend the night at his house?" he asked, and then quickly added, "His mother already said it was okay."

"Oh, well..." Kate hesitated, "you'll have to ask your Grandfather. After you eat some supper."

"Hi, Mrs. Hawkins. It's Gary. Can I talk to Frank?" Gary held the receiver close and peered around the corner into the living room, making sure he was out of earshot. "Okay, thanks..." A moment passed. "Frank? Hey, ask your mom if you can come over and spend the night... Yeah. But, wait - I'm gonna meet you half way, okay?" He listened and then rolled his eyes. "Because... Just ask her.

I'll tell you when we meet up." He waited for Frank to get permission, all the while staring at a jar of dog biscuits sitting on the pantry shelf. "Yeah? Okay, great. I'll meet you at the end of Downing in about... fifteen minutes, okay? Ride your bike." He quickly hung up the phone, praying that he hadn't been heard, and walked as casually as he could into the living room, where his grandparents sat in their respective easy chairs, Kate knitting a blanket and Roy smoking his pipe behind the newspaper.

"Frank said it's still okay if I stay over," he said.

Roy put the paper down and removed his glasses. "You know, Gary, it's okay to be sad. Leaving now isn't going to make it any easier when you come back."

"I know, I just... I'd like to go."

His grandfather sighed. "Okay. I'll get the car."

"No, uh, actually I'm just gonna ride my bike over if that's okay. We were gonna ride bikes tomorrow anyways."

Kate chimed in, "Gary, it's dark out. You know I don't like you riding on the roads after dark..."

"I'll be fine, Grandma... I promise."

Kate shot a worried glance at Roy, who seemed to be thinking intently.

"Okay?" Gary prompted.

Roy sighed again and said, "Okay, Gary. Go on."

"But, Roy," Kate interjected.

"Oh, he'll be fine, Kate. He's a big boy." Roy put his glasses back on. Gary thought he may have caught a sparkle of knowing in his grandfather's eyes, but he wasn't positive. "Have fun, Gary..."

"What the heck is goin' on, Gary?" Frank blurted as Gary rolled to a stop beneath the old elm tree at the corner of Webber and Downing. "It's freezin' out here!"

"Do you have any money?" Gary asked, his breath coming out in puffs of steam.

"What? On me? No. What's this all about?"

"Damn. All I got's a couple'a bucks..." He furrowed his brow and adjusted his knapsack. "Guess that'll have to do."

"Do for what? Gary, this suspense is killin' me!"

"Frank..." Gary said, taking a deep breath. "We're gettin' outta town."

"What?" Frank exclaimed. "Wait a min-"

"I gotta. I gotta get away from here. At least for a day. Maybe two."

Frank stood with his eyes wide, a look of confusion and incredulity painting his face. Finally, he blurted, "What the hell? What?"

Gary shushed him. "Keep it down. You're gonna wake someone up."

"What?" Frank asked again, in a whisper.

"Frank... it's Huey." Gary suddenly found it somewhat hard to speak; the words were getting held up by the lump in his throat. "He... he got hit by a car."

"Oh, no... Is he okay?"

"No. I just buried him."

"Gosh... Jeeze, I'm real sorry, Gary. That's awful."

"I know. It's pretty rough."

A moment of silence descended upon them. Finally, staring off into the distance, Frank simply said, "He was a good dog. A real good dog..."

"I know."

Frank turned back toward Gary. "But I don't understand; why are we leaving town? Where are we gonna sleep? Where are we gonna go?"

Gary sighed. "We're just gonna go. We'll have an adventure, Frankie, okay? I could use a good adventure... C'mon, let's go."

The pale moon, thinly veiled by long, wispy clouds, was their only guiding light as they headed north across the otherwise dark countryside, flanked on both sides by barren fields and sporadic patches of equally barren trees. Webber Road, with its newly blacktopped surface, passed smoothly beneath their tires.

"Maybe your grandpa an' grandma will get you another dog," Frank said, pedaling faster to catch up with Gary.

"I don't want another dog, Frank. I'll never get another one." Gary wiped at his eyes. The frigid wind that was rushing over his face was making them water.

"What? Never?"

"Never ever."

"Gosh..." Frank exclaimed quietly. "That's some kinda big statement. How come?"

Gary thought for a moment, and then said, "Frank, would you ever try to replace your mother?"

"Huh?"

"Your mom. If she ever died, would you try and find a new one?"

"Gary, that's a little different..."

"Not to me, it ain't. I've known... I knew Huey longer and better than just about anybody else in the whole wide world, and same goes for the other way around, too. He was with me through thick an' thin. No matter how bad it got, he was always there to help me through it. He knew when I was sad or mad or scared... He knew me through and through and still stuck by me." Gary let his bike coast to a stop. Frank followed suit. "He loved me, Frank... I can't replace that."

Frank fell silent for a moment, visibly deep in thought. Finally, he spoke. "Okay, but how are you ever gonna get through life thinking that way? I mean, anything that's ever gonna love you is bound to die someday."

"I'm not tryin' to get through life, Frankie. I'm tryin' to get through tonight." He adjusted his foot on the bike pedal and they slowly began moving again. "And maybe I'll have to be a little more careful of who or what I let love me, and who or what I love."

"Hmm... that sounds like a terrible idea, Gary," Frank replied, very matter-of-factly.

"Sorry. It's the best I can come up with on such short notice. Lovin' is a painful business... I just don't see the worth in it."

"Don't see the worth? Gary, what else is there? What about all the girls? What about Candy?"

"What about her? I don't love her."

Now it was Frank's turn to bring their little caravan to a halt. When his back tire finished skidding to a stop, he asked, "What'd you just say?"

"What? I don't. Sure, I *like* her alright. She makes me feel good and all, but I'd never say that I *love* her."

Frank was nearly speechless. "Gary, I can't even believe what you're sayin' right now. Candice Hauldman is like... like an angel! She's perfect! What more could you ever ask for?"

"She ain't 'perfect', Frankie, trust me. And she sure as shootin' ain't no angel. Far from it, but that's not why I don't love her."

"Why, then?"

Gary thought briefly. If he were to be completely honest, he didn't love Candy because he was afraid to love Candy. She didn't understand him. And besides, he didn't think she loved him, either. They just complimented each other well in public, and they both knew it. But he couldn't admit that to Frank. "I don't know," he shrugged. "I just don't."

Frank shook his head in disbelief. "And here I thought... So why are you even goin' steady with her? What's the point?" He suddenly sounded very disillusioned. "And how do you tell if you really love someone or not? I mean, how do you know the difference between 'love' and just 'like' a lot?"

Gary took a deep breath and let it out slowly. Frank's question came across as an earnest one, like he was genuinely trying to gather some sort of knowledge from him, knowledge that was nonexistent. He knew that Frank would take to heart whatever he said, so he had to think carefully about what he was about to be responsible for planting in his brain. He wasn't so selfish as to jeopardize Frank's relationship with Molly, no matter how much he disapproved of it, out of his own misgivings about love. "Well... I'm not really sure, Frankie. I didn't know how much I loved Huey 'till tonight, when I was laying him into his grave. I think that's one of life's cruel tricks; that you don't know what you have 'till you don't have it anymore." That probably wasn't an answer that was going to guide Frank into a better life, he realized, so he added, "But, I mean, I *did* know that I loved him all along... I just knew it." He turned to his friend. "I guess that's it: you just know, and no one can convince you otherwise."

"Hmm... Okay, but what if I'm not sure?"

"You'll be sure. Can we keep riding? We're not getting anywhere just sitting here."

"Well, maybe *you* aren't..." Frank pushed off of the pavement and began pedaling beside Gary again. "But that doesn't answer my first question."

"Which one?"

"What's the point? Of you going steady with

someone you know you don't love at all?"

"Well... I dunno. I guess I just like girls. Do you, umm... do you love your shoes?"

"Huh?"

"I know you don't love 'em. You told me so. But they come in pretty handy sometimes, don't they?"

"First you compare my Mom to your dog and now you're comparing Candy to my shoes? Gary, shoes don't have feelings. They don't care if they get used. That's a awful example."

"Candy makes me feel good, okay? That's all."

"So you're using her like a pair of shoes?"

Gary rolled his eyes. "No, I think I'm a little nicer to her than I am to my shoes."

"Well, I should hope so..."

"I'm just sayin' that I'd rather have her than not have her. That's all. And if I'm gonna have a girl, she might as well be the one that everyone says is the prettiest one around."

"What do you mean 'everyone'? You don't think she's the prettiest?"

"She's fine."

"Just 'fine'? Gary, are you blind?"

"Can we just drop this? You're happy with Molly, aren't you?"

"Well, yeah... I think so."

"Then that's all that matters. Don't worry about my problems. I'll work 'em out... What time is it?"

Frank pulled his coat sleeve back and angled his watch toward the moon. "This conversation is not over, Gary... It's about 9:30. Do you even have *any* idea where we're going?"

"Where's the fun in that?" Gary said, picking up his pace. "We've got the whole world to explore!"

The streets of Carson Creek were all but deserted, save for a handful of late night motorists that all seemed to be going the same place: Jack's All-American, the only all-night diner in town. Gary and Frank parked their bikes across the street, behind the brick form of King's Cinema.

"What are we doing here?" Frank asked.

Gary, sliding his backpack off of his shoulders, pulled a nickel from his pocket and flipped it to Frank. "You're gonna call your mama and let her know you got to my house safe and sound, before she calls my Grandparents and asks them."

Frank rolled his eyes. "Why do I let you talk me into these things..."

Beneath the pale bluish light of Main Street's lamp posts, they jogged across the road and up to Jack's, a long, low, chrome accented diner that sat neatly on the corner of Chestnut and Main, directly across the street from another one of Gary's favorite dining spots, Peppy's Pizzeria. Jack's was the local teenage hotspot for those unfortunate souls who didn't have a car to drive all the way to Willowgrove, to The Strawberry, and this was evidenced by simply peering through the neon-framed windows; the building was packed wall-to-wall with dozens of young men and women who had decided to ride out their curfews dancing along with the shiny new jukebox or sharing a frosty Cherry Coke float, which, according to the sign in the window, was Jack's specialty.

The door jingled as Gary pushed it open. He and Frank were immediately assaulted by a heady concoction of hamburger grease, cigarette smoke and over-applied perfumes, married with the bouncy, twangy strains of Les Paul and Mary Ford's *'How High the Moon'* pouring from the Wurlitzer. A long, horseshoe-shaped island bar stretched through the center of the diner, surrounded by swiveling stools supporting all manner of patrons; preps, greasers, hot-rodders and a few misplaced-looking young men in military uniforms, all of whom were laughing and carrying on while sampling various delectables from Jack's menu. As Gary led Frank toward the far corner, where a wooden phone booth stood, conversations seemed to die down in his wake. He heard people whispering *"That's that kid..."* and *"He's the one that saved the Mayor's daughter..."* and *"Isn't that Gary Bell?"* He thought he may have even heard a snippet of conversation containing the words 'The Lone Wolf'. Still not used to the attention he'd begun to receive following his escapade at Whitefeather, having been a front page headline in three separate newspapers, he bowed his head and quickened his pace, suddenly feeling uncomfortably vulnerable. The last thing he needed were people inquiring about his present activities. They reached the phone booth and stepped inside, with Gary hastily pulling the door shut behind them.

"Now... what am I supposed to say again?" Frank asked, his voice muffled by the small space.

"Just tell 'er you made it to my house alright. And that you're gonna be spending all day tomorrow with me, too."

Frank shook his head slowly, letting out a sigh as he pushed the nickel into the slot and began turning the rotor.

As Frank started his charade, Gary aimlessly turned his attention to the large cork board hanging in the booth, which was plastered with dozens of notes, announcements, important phone numbers and various other bits of local information. One in particular caught Gary's eye. It was pinned directly in the center of the board, covering a large portion, and was crisp and clean, appearing newer than the other posts. He took a step closer to examine its hand-written message. The header, in bold pencil, read: 'REWARD!' followed by smaller, wobbly cursive,

'Lost puppy - Female Beagle - Small, White/Brown fur, Brown collar - last seen near Henline Corners, East of Willowgrove on 4/9 - comes to the name 'Becky' - please contact Mr. J. Gabriel Kelly with any information regarding her whereabouts - $10 reward for her safe return - Call: Union-0905.'

A pang of sorrow shot through Gary's stomach, not necessarily for the lost dog, but for being reminded of his own canine friend. The previous fall, Huey had disappeared for an entire week, and it had nearly killed Gary with worry; unable to eat, to sleep, to focus on his schoolwork, or on anything else for that matter, those seven days had drug on like some horrible, inescapable nightmare. It was awful. He'd never forget the deluge of relief that swept over him when Huey, bedraggled and limping, appeared at the end of the lane, looking as if he'd just come from the battlefield. All of that seemed so far away now. Huey was lost for good, and as much as he wished to the contrary, Gary knew that his old friend wouldn't be reappearing at the end of the driveway this time.

The more he allowed himself to remember, the more he began to feel an uncanny connection with this Mr. J. Gabriel Kelly and his pup Becky. If Huey had just disappeared and never came back Gary would probably have gone crazy in the uncertainty, not knowing the final fate of his friend, and if Becky was loved half as much as Huey had been, then she was being sorely missed. He was surprised by the desire that was slowly beginning to grow in him, the desire to help this unknown man find his lost puppy. The sound of Frank hanging up the receiver brought him out of his reverie.

"Okay, there. I told her," Frank said, sounding

slightly perturbed. "Now what?"

Gary continued to gaze at the cork board. "How'd you like to make five bucks, Frankie?"

"Huh? How?"

"This." He pointed to the handwritten note, tapping it with his finger.

Frank leaned over and began to read the message out loud.

"It's a reward for a lost dog," Gary interrupted. "Ten bucks. We could split it fifty-fifty."

"But..." Frank finished reading silently. "What makes you think we could find a lost dog? In Willowgrove, to boot?"

Gary thought for a moment, for the first time taking into consideration the difficulty of what he was proposing. After all, he hadn't been able to find Huey when he was lost, and he'd spent every minute of daylight trying to do so, but for some reason he felt a magnetic draw to the task. He couldn't explain it to himself, let alone to Frank. "Can't be that hard," he offered, trying to sound convincing. "I've been up that way quite a bit with Gramps. He owns some fields up there, so I know my way around."

"I don't know..."

"C'mon, it'll be an adventure. That's just what we're lookin' for, right? And we could even pick up some quick dough at the same time."

"But that's gotta be ten miles away, Gary. You wanna ride our bikes all the-" Frank was interrupted by a sharp rap on the phone booth's glass door. They turned to see a tough-looking greaser in his late teens waiting to use the phone, chewing on a candy cane-striped straw and flipping a nickel with his thumb.

"We'll figure it all out on the way," Gary said, pulling Frank by the elbow. He glanced back at Mr. Kelly's phone number one last time. "C'mon, let's get outta here."

As they hopped back on their bikes and pointed them north, Gary began to grow excited. Slowly but surely, his deep sadness was ebbing away and being replaced with the thrill of the hunt, of exploration, of a new adventure. He would do this in Huey's honor, he decided. He couldn't think of a more fitting task to commemorate the passing of his friend than to reunite another person with their own dog. If he could pull it off. He still wasn't sure how he was going to go about locating the lost pup, but conceded that he'd think of something when the time came.

"Gary, I don't know if I can ride all this way. Ten miles is pretty far. And it's cold out here..."

"Aww, don't be a baby. Just pedal faster. It'll keep you warm."

"This is gonna take... hours. I can't keep pedaling fast for hours. I'd probably get a heart attack."

Gary rolled his eyes. "Judas Priest, Frank..."

"Maybe we could just go home. And then come back and do this tomorrow."

"No, no... we're already committed."

"We are?"

"Yeah. C'mon, Frankie! Where's your spirit of adventure?" Gary said, slapping his handlebars. "We're like Lewis and Clark! Or Jules Verne or something..." As they passed beneath one of the street lamp's spotlights, Frank's illuminated expression of doubt came into view. Gary sighed. "Alright, look... Gramps has a bunch'a land just outside of town, with some old barns. We can ride that far tonight and then finish in the morning, okay? We can stay the night in one of the barns."

Frank took a deep breath, contemplating the proposal. When he didn't reply, Gary prompted again.

"And how about this... I just thought of it; the train tracks run in back of the fields there. We can hop on the train in the morning and ride it all the way to Willowgrove, no pedaling. How's *that* for a plan, huh?"

"But how are we gonna get on a moving train? Isn't that dangerous?"

"Jiminy *Christmas*, Frank!" Gary exclaimed, throwing his head back in exasperation. "Just trust me for once, will ya? Have I ever steered you wrong before?"

"Well..."

"No. I haven't."

"But what about throwin' eggs at Mrs. Rokissian's car? That got us in a heap'a trouble..."

"That's just 'cause you had to go and fess up to it. That was *your* fault... And even then it was still worth it." Gary smiled to himself, recalling the incident, and then turned back toward Frank. "And this is a totally different situation. We're actually gonna *help* somebody this time. How can we get in trouble for helping somebody?"

"Well... I guess so..."

"Gosh, I get tired'a of havin' to talk you into things all the time..."

"Well, maybe if your ideas weren't so crazy all the time, you wouldn't have to. How come you can't just be a normal kid with normal ideas? Why do you always hafta come up with these harebrained schemes?" Frank asked, an ever-so-thin tinge of anger and disdain coming through his voice.

Gary bristled at the question, feeling somewhat hurt that his so-called 'best friend' didn't approve of his admittedly reckless lifestyle. "Because that's what I'm like," he snapped, "an' I ain't changin' it for nobody. *Nobody*, you hear?"

"Alright, alright," Frank immediately replied in a calming tone, "No need to get sore. I was only askin'."

"An' I was only tellin'. If somebody don't like me, they can pound salt. I don't care what anybody thinks about who I am or what I do. I don't care if-"

"Okay, okay, I get it," Frank interrupted, "I'm glad you're like you are, okay? Simmer down..."

Gary forced himself to take Frank's advice, slowly. He didn't need to lose another friend at the moment. "Fine."

"How far is this barn you're talkin' about?"

"It's... just about a mile outside of town. Not far..."

They soon left Main Street behind, turning onto Porter Road, which slowly began to cut in a northeast direction as they pedaled through the gently rolling, moonlit fields that filled the nearly ten mile gap between the low laying Carson Creek and its closest neighbor, Willowgrove, which sat high atop Eastlake Ridge. The temperature continued to drop, and Gary's face was beginning to burn from the added chill brought on by his quick pace. He wiped the water from his eyes.

"It's right up here," he said, "on the left." He pointed to a dirt lane that shot off the main road and disappeared over a small hill, cutting through the field.

"Does it got hot and cold running water?" Frank laughed.

"Not at the same time. There's a creek that runs in back of the barn, next to the railroad tracks. It's probably cold running water tonight." Gary turned his bike to lead the way down the bumpy dirt road.

"Your grandpappy owns all this?" Frank asked, his voice bouncing as they traversed the rough ground.

"Yep. And a bunch more. He inherited it from my Great Grandpa. Over three hundred acres."

"Wow... How's he take care of it all?"

"Rents it out, mostly. He's got some gas wells out here, too."

"You're gonna be all set when you grow up, you know."

"Yeah... I guess that's one thing I have to look forward to... The barn's right over this hill..."

"I'm sure gonna miss him..." Gary said wistfully, gazing intently into the small campfire that they had built using twigs and small branches from the trees that surrounded the barn, helped along with some dry straw they'd pulled out of the bales in the loft. He held his hands out to warm them. "I always hoped this day would never come."

"Yeah..." Frank replied. He sat propped up against a stump, eyes trained on the stars. "I'm gonna miss him, too." They were silent for a long moment and then Frank asked, "Do you think dogs go to heaven?"

"Why wouldn't they?"

"I dunno. I just never thought about it."

"Well, if they don't, then I'm goin' to hell."

"Don't say that..."

"Listen, Huey was a better person than anybody I know, so if he ain't gettin' in, nobody is."

Frank sat up, looking serious. "I'm not goin' to hell. You can go there if you want to, but I ain't."

Gary waved him off. "Psshh, Frankie... You're too good to go to hell anyways. They wouldn't even know what to do with you down there. Me, on the other hand... I'm not even gonna worry about it. I plan on livin' life to the fullest. Enjoyin' every bit of it. I mean, I'm not gonna hurt anybody, but I'm also not gonna live my life bein' a pussy, scared about a bunch'a little red men with pitchforks..."

"Holy Moses, Gary... if your granny could hear you right now..."

"Yeah, well... I love Grandma Kate to death, but she's way too uptight for my taste. All she does is worry all the time. Pisses me right off. Like the other day when I accidentally said 'shit' in front of her. I thought she was gonna dig me a hole straight to hell herself."

Frank broke into a laugh. "What? I can't believe you said 'shit' in front of your grandma..."

"Why? It's just a word. Shit, bitch, ass... they're all just stupid words that people like you and me made up and decided they'd be 'bad'. It's stupid. I can do the same thing with any word I want to. Tell me who decided 'shit' was a bad word and 'crap' wasn't, will ya? They both mean the same thing, right?"

"I guess I never thought of it that way..."

"And that's the problem, Frankie; nobody thinks for themselves anymore. Like my Grandma; she just takes everything she's always been taught as the gospel truth." He leaned forward and pointed to his head. "You gotta think about stuff. Use your brain. Use some common sense. Don't just be some dumb sheep your whole life, stuck behind a fence that isn't really there."

Frank stared blankly at Gary for a moment and then laid back down. "Wow... I... Where'd you learn all this?"

"I learned it by opening my eyes and ears, Frank. By not bein' scared of questioning things. I don't wanna live in a perfect little bubble, spendin' every day scared to death that it's gonna pop, and you shouldn't, either."

"Well... I don't."

"Yeah you do..."

"No, I mean I don't want to, either. I wanna be able to think for myself, enjoy life... all that stuff. How do you do it?"

"You just gotta be yourself, Frank. Be a man. Don't care what anyone else thinks, don't even care what *I* think. Live without bein' scared of makin' mistakes, break some rules every now and then. Mainly, don't be scared'a *nothin'*."

"Hmm... Sounds easier said than done."

"Nah, it just takes a little practice. You'll get the hang of it." Gary reached into his backpack and drew out a small canteen. After taking a sip, he tossed it over the fire to Frank. "Don't worry; it's just water."

Frank sniffed it and then took a swig. "You don't got any blankets in there, do you?" he asked, shivering as he pulled his jacket collar up.

"As a matter of fact..." Gary reached back in and tugged out a neatly rolled, olive green army blanket.

Frank laughed. "You don't happen to have *two* blankets in there, do you?"

"No... here," he said, throwing Frank the blanket. "I don't need it."

"You sure?"

"Yeah, it ain't that bad out. I'll just sleep by the fire."

"Well, I think I'm gonna hit the hay... for real." Frank smiled. "An' I'm gonna think about what you said."

"Okay, pal... 'night." Gary watched as Frank gathered up the blanket and withdrew to the barn. Turning back to the crackling fire, he wondered if he was really as fearless as he made himself out to be.

"Frank...! Frank! Wake up!" Gary reached down and shook his friend, who lay burrowed in a nest of straw like a field mouse.

Frank snorted himself into consciousness. "W-what's happening...? Where am I?"

"C'mon. It's time to go."

"What? Where?" Frank rubbed his eyes vigorously.

"We're goin' for a train ride, pal..." Gary turned and made his way back out of the barn to admire his handiwork. The sun, shining brightly through the pristine blue sky, warmed his bare hands as he shielded his eyes and gazed out across the field to the railroad tracks, where a massive pile of straw bales sat in a neat pyramid, directly in the path of any train that would happen to come along. Gary figured that if it didn't stop them, it would surely slow them down. He glanced over his shoulder to see Frank stumble out of the barn, still wrapped in the army blanket.

"What the..." Frank exclaimed, squinting in the sunlight. "Did you do that?"

"Couldn't sleep. What's the time?"

Frank rubbed his eyes again and looked at his watch. "Ten after seven."

"Near as I can tell, the train should be along any minute. We'll hafta leave our bikes here." As if to punctuate Gary's prediction, a train whistle blew off in the distance. "C'mon, we can hide in the trees over there," he said, pulling his knapsack on.

No sooner had they settled into their hiding spot in the creek side weeds, about fifty feet from the tracks, a white, streaming plume of steam appeared in the distance, followed by the familiar 'chugging' sound of the old locomotive. Gary watched intently as the freight train rounded a corner and came into full view, cutting through the fields like an iron serpent.

"Okay, this is it," he said, maneuvering into position.

"Stay down 'till the engine passes, then follow me."

Frank smiled. "I feel like a train robber..."

"Well, maybe they call you 'Freight Train Frankie' for more than just your snoring..."

"Yeah, maybe."

Gary glanced at the straw barricade and then turned his attention back to the train. It was getting close, and he had yet to hear the brakes come on.

"Gary... I don't think..."

"You know... I think you're right..." Gary replied, jumping up. "We're gonna have to run for it. C'mon!" He leapt from the weeds and began sprinting across the field, with Frank on his heels. As he ran, Gary watched as the engine hit the bales of straw without slowing a bit, the pyramid exploding upon impact into a huge plume of yellow confetti.

"Where's the caboose?" Frank yelled. "There's no caboose!"

"I know, I know! Just... head for that last boxcar!"

"This is a bad idea!"

"Run faster!" Gary yelled over the 'clickety-clack' of the cars. If they didn't reach the train before it passed, they'd never be able to keep up with it. Luckily for them, it wasn't at full speed yet, having just passed through Carson Creek. "Go for the ladder!"

"On the back?"

"Yeah!" The final car, a weathered red box, began passing in front of them. Gary pumped his legs as fast as they would go and leapt for the ladder at the rear, swinging around the corner, just barely wrapping his fingertips around one of the rungs. He struggled to hang on. "C'mon! Jump!" he called over his shoulder as he finally secured his grip.

"I... can't... reach!" Frank huffed, slowly falling behind.

"Gimme your hand!"

With a grunt, Frank jumped, arm outstretched and aiming for Gary's open palm.

Gary caught him by the wrist. The weight nearly ripped him off of the ladder. "Put your feet on the ladder!" he yelled, doing his best to maintain his grip on both Frank and the boxcar. "Grab it!"

"Argggh-got it! I got it!"

Relieved, Gary retightened his hold on the ladder and began climbing to the roof. With one final push, he thrust himself over the top, sprawling out on his back. Frank soon followed.

"That..." Frank managed as they both lay panting, "was crazy. *Completely*... crazy."

Gary, his heart feeling as if it was about to come through his chest, rolled onto his side and began laughing between his gasps. "Yeah... maybe that time... I was... a little crazy..."

Frank joined in the laughter. "I don't... I don't think your roadblock... worked."

"Me either... Next time... I'll set it on fire." He laid still until he caught his breath and then sat up, sighing heavily. "But we made it."

"We're on our way!"

With the brisk, but welcome, breeze rushing over him, Gary gazed out across the gently rolling countryside, now passing by at a much faster clip than it would have been were they still pedaling. His thoughts turned back to the task ahead. "Yep. On our way..."

"Uhh... Gary...?"

Gary, who had been stretched out, basking in the warm sun, turned to see an alarmed-looking Frank pointing toward the front of the train. "What?"

"Look..."

He followed Franks direction, but couldn't see the front of the train; it was quickly disappearing into a tunnel. A very narrow, very low-ceilinged tunnel. "Jeepers creepers... I forgot about that..."

"You *forgot?*"

"Yeah..."

"Well," Frank began to panic, "what are we gonna do?"

Gary's heart began to pound again, but he forced himself to remain calm enough to think. The tunnel was nearly upon them; they didn't have time to scramble to the ladder, having moved toward the front of the boxcar. They either had to jump or... "Lay down! Flat as you can!"

"*What?* We're gonna get peeled off like scabs! In fact, that's all we're *gonna* be!"

"Lay down!" Gary ordered again, pressing himself out as flush with the roof as possible.

"Jesus, Joseph and Mary!" Frank yelled as he followed Gary's lead. "We're gonna die!"

Gary squeezed his eyes shut, bracing for impact in the unfortunate event that he had miscalculated how tall the steam engine's exhaust stack was in relation to the freight cars. He turned his head sideways. The echoing roar of the train being swallowed by the hillside rushed toward them like the unrelenting call of a savage beast. "Hang on!" he yelled, eyes still shut.

"We're gonna die!" Frank repeated.

The sound grew to a deafening pitch and Gary felt a *whoosh* pass over his body. Daylight disappeared. His brain rattled with the echoing cacophony of jostling cars, clunking wheels and the steady *chug chug chug* of the engine, all amplified in the tight space. Hot, suppressing steam washed over him. He hadn't died yet. Slightly relieved, he allowed himself a peek, but may as well have kept his eyes shut; the tunnel was pitch black. He slowly reached into his jacket pocket and pulled out his wind-proof Zippo, flicking it to life. He stiffened. About eight inches from his face, the brick ceiling of the tunnel was passing overhead in a blur. "Keep your eyes shut, Frank!" he yelled, flipping the lighter closed, unsure if his friend could even hear him over the raucous noise. "We're gonna be okay! Just stay still!"

"I ain't movin' a muscle!" came Frank's faint reply.

Gary felt trapped, helpless. All he could do was grit his teeth and ride it out, all the while questioning every decision he'd made that had led them there. Then he remembered something his grandfather had said on multiple occasions, that when it comes to making decisions, always choose the one that will make for the best story later on. He'd certainly done that.

After what seemed like an hour, another *whoosh* swept over them, and the sound finally broke free of the tunnel. The blinding sun stabbed Gary in the eyes as he tried to gain his bearings. It took a moment for his vision to adjust, but when it did he saw that they had made it to the other side of Eastlake Ridge. The train was sandwiched between a steep hill bristling with tall pines on the left side and a dirt roadway on the right. Beyond the road, the heavily wooded land gently sloped downward, and farther east of that, past the trees, fields could be seen off in the distance.

"Frank! You can open your eyes now," Gary said, laughing. "We're almost there."

"We're alive...?"

"Yes, we're alive, you baby. Henline Corners is right up there." He pointed. "We'll slow down in a minute."

Sure enough, the train began to scrub off speed as it

rounded a bend and the high-pitched squeal of the brakes reached their ears. Gary slipped his backpack on.

"Aren't we gonna wait for the train to stop?" Frank asked.

"Then we'd have to walk all the way back here," Gary replied. "It's not stoppin' right now, anyways. It's just slowin' down. Don't worry; gettin' off is a lot easier than gettin' on."

"Yeah, I'll bet..."

"C'mon," Gary said, standing, "I'll go first." He made his way back to the ladder and began to ease himself down. Beneath him, the tracks were still whizzing by at about fifteen miles per hour. He looked back up at Frank, who was waiting at the top of the ladder. "Alright," he yelled, "just get to the last rung, turn around, and then jump off, okay? Watch me." He took a deep breath and maneuvered around so that he was facing away from the boxcar. Without allowing himself any time to lose his nerve, he jumped, hitting the wooden railroad ties with a grunt. He stumbled a bit, but stuck the landing and turned around to watch Frank, who was still making his way down the ladder. "Hurry up!" he yelled, cupping his hands around his mouth. He ran, trying to keep up. "Jump!"

Frank seemed to be hesitating.

"Jump!" Gary repeated. He watched as his friend squeezed his eyes shut and leapt from the train, soaring haphazardly through the air with his arms flailing in all directions. Not very graceful, Gary thought. Frank landed off balance with a thud and tumbled off of the tracks, down the short gravel retaining hill and out into the middle of the dirt road, where he came to rest spread eagle, staring up at the sky. When he didn't move, Gary became concerned. "Frank?" he called, sliding down the hill. "You okay?"

Frank groaned. His eyes were still shut tight. "Saint

Peter? Is that you?"

"What the hell was *that?*" Gary exclaimed, leaning over Frank. "Who taught you how to jump off a movin' train?"

"You did," Frank replied, coughing. "You're a *awful* teacher."

"Well, I didn't tell you to close your eyes! Jeeze... Hey, you're bleeding..."

"What?" Frank began looking himself over.

"On your head. Looks like you scraped it."

"You know..." Frank said, feeling his forehead. "I don't even care anymore. I'm just glad we're off that *stupid* train."

Gary helped him stand, brushing some dirt off of his jacket. "Me too. Now we can get to work."

"Work? After that whole ordeal, all I wanna do is go back to sleep!"

"Aww, c'mon. It wasn't that bad."

"Yeah, I guess we only *almost* died three times... Where are we goin' now, anyways?"

Gary looked down the road in both directions. Not seeing any signs that read 'go here for lost dogs', he pointed to the trees in front of them. "I guess this is as good a place as any to start..."

The next several hours were spent wandering aimlessly through the woods, zig-zagging back and forth between the roadway and the fields, all the while whistling and calling 'Becky!' and 'Here, girl!', to no avail. The trees overhead were still largely barren, with the only exceptions being the old oaks that had held onto their leaves through the long, cold winter. The soft ground was littered with compost and sporadic patches of briars and various other forms of woodland ground foliage, which, at times, made for difficult navigation.

Smacking through some bushes with a stick he'd found, Frank grumbled, "I'm hungry, Gary. Didn't you bring any food?"

"No. And I forgot to bring my crybaby spray, too," Gary replied, clambering over a fallen tree.

"It's gotta be after lunchtime." Frank looked at his watch. "Yeah, it is."

"Well, we're gonna have to skip lunch."

"What about supper?"

Gary sighed. "Is eating all you think about? Look, if we haven't found the dog by supper time, we'll go back to the road and walk down to The Strawberry. It's only a couple'a miles back. Okay? I still got a few bucks."

"Okay... I guess." Frank said reluctantly. "I don't think we're ever gonna find this stupid dog anyways..."

"Not with that attitude, we won't. You gotta have a little faith, Frankie."

Frank stopped. "Gary, can't you see that this whole idea is just one big wild goose chase? The odds of finding a lost dog out here are prob'ly a... a hundred to one. The paper said it'd been missing since the 9th... that was *five* days ago. Heck, somebody's prob'ly already found her! Or maybe she's dead already! Or drowned or something! There's absolutely no way of knowing that we're not just out here wasting our time!" Having worked himself into a fit, he collapsed to the ground, cradling his head in his hands. "This whole idea was crazy. We should just go home..."

Before he could clobber Frank over the head with his own walking stick, something caught Gary's eye. "Frank... you're a genius..."

"I know! So how come you never-"

"Look!" Gary interrupted, pointing to the ground at Frank's feet.

"What?"

"Tracks! Paw prints! *Puppy* paw prints!" Gary stooped down to examine them. They ran directly under Frank, shallow depressions in the soft ground that disappeared into the bushes. "Get up, you're sittin' on 'em!"

"How did..."

"You found 'em!" Gary exclaimed, knowing full well that it was pure coincidence; he was trying to rekindle his friend's commitment to the task.

"I did...?"

"Yeah! C'mon, they go that way... let's follow 'em!"

For another two hours, they traced the paw prints for what seemed like miles. Sometimes the tracks doubled back, sometimes they appeared crisp and fresh, and other times they disappeared altogether, in which case Gary and Frank would have to search the area until they picked up the trail again. It was in one of these searches that Frank began to grow weary for the second time.

"How do we even know this is the right dog? I mean, there's gotta be tons of dogs around here..."

"It's the right dog. The prints are small. They're from a puppy."

"It could just be another small dog. Or another puppy, even."

"Look! Found 'em again." Gary said, pushing through some bushes.

"Great... Yay..."

"Oh, quit whinin'. What else would you be doing today that could possibly be more important than this?"

"I could be at home, nice and warm, safe and sound, and *not* hungry. I could be reading about stuff like this instead of actually doing it. I could be playing a game inside or doing homework."

"Homework? Really, Frank?"

"Okay, I wouldn't be doing homework... but I'd be doing other things."

"Becky!" Gary bellowed. "Here, girl!" He turned back to Frank. "We're doin' this in honor of Huey, Frank."

"We are?"

"Yeah. We are."

"You're sure we're not just doin' it so you can run away from feelin' bad about Huey? So you can keep yourself from bein' sad?"

Gary stopped. "What's that supposed to mean?"

"Nothin'. Forget it."

They continued on in silence for another hour. Gary was so lost in his thoughts that he barely noticed the faint whimpering coming from the briar patch ahead of them.

"Shh..." Frank hushed, stopping. "Did you hear that?"

"Yeah... I did."

"Do you think...?"

"Could be..." Gary began to grow excited. "Only one way to find out." He quietly took a few steps closer to the bushes, noticing that the paw prints ran directly inside. He glanced back at Frank, who was watching intently, and then returned his attention to the briars. Using a stick, he pushed aside the thick branches and peered inside. There, curled in a shivering ball, lay Becky. Her brown leather collar had gotten caught in the branches. "Becky...?" Gary said quietly. She looked up at him and began to wag her tail. "I found her Frank! I mean, *we* found her!"

"Really? Is she okay?" Frank asked, quickly coming

to investigate.

"Looks okay. See? I told you!" Gary laughed, slapping Frank on the back. "She got tangled! Here, help me get her out... Hold these briars back..." With Frank's assistance, Gary stooped down and unbuckled Becky's collar, getting his arms and face scratched by the thorns in the process. "Ouch! Okay, got it!"

As soon as she was free, the small brown and white pup bolted out of the thorn bush and began running and jumping around Gary and Frank, barking hoarsely with pure, unbridled joy.

Gary knelt down to pet her and she jumped on him and began licking his face, nearly knocking him over. "Whoa!" he said, laughing.

She traded Gary for Frank, repeating the process.

"She's prob'ly thirsty," Gary said, slipping off his knapsack. He pulled out the canteen. "Here... cup your hands together." Frank did so and Gary poured a small amount of water into them, which Becky quickly lapped up. She continued to do so until the canteen was completely empty.

"She *was* thirsty," Frank said.

"Who knows how long she was stuck in there... Days, maybe."

"Now what do we do?"

"Well, we need to get to a phone somehow," Gary replied, patting Becky on the head. "I guess we'll have to walk back to The Strawberry. That's the closest place I know of."

"I still can't believe we actually found her... out of all the places she could have been lost. She prob'ly would'a died out here."

"I guess it was just meant to be, Frankie..." Gary said, standing. "You ready to go, Becky? Huh, girl?"

Becky began wagging her tail vigorously, jumping up

on her hind legs.

Gary laughed. "Alright, let's get you home..."

As luck would have it, they didn't have to walk the three miles back to The Strawberry; no sooner had they begun in that direction, an old farm truck came bouncing down the dirt road toward them. Gary waved for it to stop, which it did. The driver, a kindly-looking, middle-aged man wearing overalls and leather work gloves, leaned over and rolled the passenger window down.

"How kin I help you fellas?" the man asked.

"Hi," Gary said. "Can you take us to a telephone?"

"Why, sure! Hop on in. That's a pretty pup you got there. You kin put her in the back."

"Actually, it's not mine. We found 'er, my friend and me." Gary motioned toward Frank. "We gotta call her owner."

"Oh, I see. Okay, well hop in. I'll run you up to Kelly's place. He's only a mile or so up the road a piece. He's got a telephone."

"Kelly?" Gary asked incredulously. "Mr. J. Gabriel Kelly?"

"That's the man's name, sure."

Gary turned to Frank, smiling from ear to ear. "Told ya it was meant to be..."

"Okay, thanks again, Mr. Mainer!" Gary said, gathering Becky out of the truck bed. They had been brought to the driveway of a large, cream-colored house surrounded by ancient oak trees.

"Anytime, boys. Tell yer grandpa I said 'howdy', Gary."

"Sure will! Thanks!" Gary waved with his free hand,

holding Becky in the other. He watched as the truck sped off and then turned toward the house. "I guess this is it, Frankie. Maybe he'll give us a ride home..."

"I sure hope so. I don't feel like I can walk another two feet."

"Well, you gotta at least make it to the front door. C'mon." Gary led the way up the gravel driveway and unto the front porch, still holding Becky, who, judging by her excitement, clearly knew where she was.

"I hope he's home," Frank said, ringing the doorbell. "I don't see any cars around."

But a moment later, they heard footsteps approaching the door. The drapes in the window parted, revealing a weathered-looking man in his mid to late fifties. Upon seeing Becky, the man's pale brown eyes instantly teared up. He swung the door open.

"Mr. Kelly?" Gary said, handing Becky over. "I think we found something that belongs to you."

"Yes... Yes, I believe you have," Mr. Kelly choked. "Becky Lou!"

Becky immediately began licking away her master's tears of joy, wagging her tail like there was no tomorrow.

"Where," he asked between puppy kisses, "where did you find her?"

"Down that way." Gary pointed. "In the woods. She got her collar caught in a briar bush. We gave her some water, but she's prob'ly still thirsty."

"Yes, of course! Come in, come in..." Mr. Kelly stepped aside so that Gary and Frank could enter. "I can't even begin to tell you how relieved I am. Thank you boys, from the bottom of my heart. You don't have any idea what she means to me..."

Gary stepped into the spacious foyer, wiping his feet on the floor mat. The inside of the house was an impressive sight; brilliant hardwood floors, vaulted ceilings, expensive-looking paintings on the wall, and all of it was immaculate. He felt like he was entering a museum.

"Go on in, make yourself at home." Mr. Kelly said, shutting the door behind them. "Can I offer you boys something to drink?"

"Sure," Gary replied, nodding to Frank.

"Lemonade okay?"

"Sounds great."

"Come on in the kitchen. What are your names?" he asked, leading them deeper into the house, with Becky still in his arms.

"I'm Gary. This is my friend Frank. We live down in Carson Creek, where we saw your note posted at Jack's." They entered the large kitchen.

"Well, Gary and Frank, you can't even begin to imagine how much this little pup means to me. I'd almost given up hope. Have a seat at the table." He finally sat Becky down and opened the refrigerator, pulling out a pitcher of lemonade. He then grabbed two glasses out of the cupboard and sat them in front of Gary and Frank. "There you go," he said, pouring them each a tall glassful.

"Thank you," they both replied in unison. Gary took a long drink; it was delicious.

"No, thank you. A thousand times over." Mr. Kelly sat the pitcher down and pulled out a chair for himself. Becky jumped up on his lap. "You see, Becky Lou here was my wife's puppy. She wanted one so bad, so I got her one last Christmas..." His voice broke slightly, but he quickly regained his composure. "Well, she passed away about a month ago, so... Becky is all I have left."

"Wow... I'm sorry," Gary said.

"Yeah..." Frank replied.

"Well, boys... that's life. Things happen."

"Don't you have any kids?" Gary asked.

Mr. Kelly pursed his lips. "Yes... I did. I had a son, but he was killed in France during the war."

"My dad got it in France, too," Frank said, "in '44..."

Mr. Kelly nodded. "That was the same year as my Bobby. June 6th; D-day. He was in the first wave to hit the beaches."

"Wow..." Gary exclaimed quietly.

"He was a good boy, too. Had a bright future." He suddenly stood up. "Here, I'll show you." He motioned them to follow.

They stood and were led into an adjoining room, full of pictures and glass cabinets, which were loaded with what looked like hundreds of trophies and awards.

"These were all his..." Mr. Kelly said.

Gary stepped up to one of the cabinets. The brilliant, glistening trophies inside were for several different types of achievements; football, baseball, bowling, track and field, but the vast majority of them were for an entirely different kind of sport, one that immediately caught his attention: motorcycle racing. "He... raced motorcycles?"

Mr. Kelly nodded. "Indeed he did, much to his mother's protests. He was a three time national champion, a veritable trophy machine." He smiled softly to himself, shaking his head. "He would've been world champion many times over, no doubt." He moved to the wall and pulled a picture down. "Here he is with his bike."

"Wow..." Gary gasped, taking the picture. It showed a ruggedly handsome Bobby Kelly, beaming, holding a massive trophy in one arm, and the trophy girl in the other, while sitting astride a heavily modified racing bike. "What kinda motorcycle is that?"

"Indian. That's all he ever raced. That one was a '39, I believe."

"Wow..." Gary said again, handing the picture to Frank. "What happened to it?"

Mr. Kelly smiled. "You want to see it?"

"Boy, do I!"

"Come on. They're all out in the garage."

Mr. Kelly, with Becky tagging along behind him, led the way out the back door and up to a large, two car garage that sat behind the house. He pushed the door up.

"They're back in the corner. Under that tarp," he said, switching on the lights.

Gary, with Frank behind him, made his way between a gleaming new sedan and an equally nice pick-up truck to the back of the garage, stopping in front of the dusty tarp. Mr. Kelly gently tugged it away for them, revealing four motorcycles, each one lower and leaner than the last.

"Holy... Moses," Gary said, in awe. "They're beautiful."

"Well, they could use a bath," Mr. Kelly chuckled. "They've been sitting here for over ten years. I turn them over by hand every few months, just so the engines don't seize up."

Gary ran his fingers over the handlebars of the bike he'd seen in the picture. It looked even faster and more menacing in person. It had been stripped down to next to nothing; no fenders, no lights and no side panels. All that seemed to remain were wheels and an engine. He was in love. "What are you gonna do with 'em?" he asked.

"Oh, I'm getting ready to sell them, along with everything else. I'm moving to Florida soon to live with my sister. I can't afford to keep this place any longer and I certainly don't need all of this space for just myself. And as much as I'd love to do so, taking these bikes with me just isn't feasible."

"You're selling 'em? How much?" Gary asked.

Mr. Kelly smiled. "Oh, I don't know... I'm not sure if

they have much more than sentimental value anymore. As I said, they've been sitting for quite some time."

"How much is sentimental value worth? I got three bucks in my pocket!" Gary blurted, yanking the cash out and holding it up. He couldn't help himself.

"I see that," Mr. Kelly chuckled again, a little harder this time. "I'll have to let you know when I'm ready to sell them..." He began recovering the bikes.

Crestfallen, Gary slowly shoved the cash back in his pocket. He almost felt like he was going to cry, again unable to help himself. The immediate attraction to the '39 was almost instinctive, something he couldn't explain, and even though he'd only seen it for a few seconds, he already felt like he was saying goodbye to an old friend. His glassy eyes met Mr. Kelly's for a moment.

"Although..." Mr. Kelly said, stopping, having noticed Gary's change in demeanor. He thought for a moment, and his face softened into a gentle, almost sad, smile. "I did offer a twenty dollar reward, didn't I?"

Gary thought it was only ten, but he didn't say anything, instead he just nodded.

"And that makes twenty three with the money in your pocket..." He bent down and scooped up Becky. "What do you think, Becky Lou?"

Becky began licking him again.

"Well... I suppose I could let it go for twenty three... assuming the buyer was going to love and take care of it like Bobby did and give it a good home."

Gary could scarcely believe his ears. "Oh, he would alright!" he almost yelled.

"And assuming that same buyer would be responsible and wait until he was old enough to ride it and not go and get himself killed when the time came..."

"No... no, sir, he wouldn't get himself killed!" Gary looked at Frank, who didn't appear nearly excited enough, in his opinion.

"You promise?" Mr. Kelly asked, holding out his hand.

"Cross my heart an' hope to die, I do!" Gary said, nearly shaking the man's hand right off of his arm.

"Okay, okay..." Mr. Kelly laughed. "But you boys are going to have to load it in the truck. My back won't stand for that sort of thing anymore."

Again, Gary felt as if he were about to cry, but this time out of pure joy. "That's... That's no problem at all! We can do that, can't we, Frank?"

"Yeah, sure... we can do that." Frank replied, sounding a bit unenthusiastic.

"Oh, here," Gary said, pulling the three crumpled one dollar bills from his pocket and handing them to Mr. Kelly. "I almost forgot!"

Mr. Kelly smiled. "Okay, Gary... Thank you."

"Thank *you!*"

"Let's get her loaded up, and I'll take you boys home. How's that sound?"

"Sounds great! C'mon, Frankie!"

"You're sure you want me to stop here?" Mr. Kelly asked, having pulled the pick-up off to the side of Webber Road, at the corner of Downing.

"Yeah, this is perfect," Gary replied. He didn't want his grandparents knowing about the bike just yet. "I'll just walk it home from here. My Grandma takes naps in the late afternoon, an' I don't wanna wake her up..." He glanced at Frank, who had been strangely quiet the entire ride home.

"Well, okay," Mr. Kelly said, cutting the ignition. "If you're sure you can handle it."

"Oh, sure. We'll be alright." Gary hopped out of the truck and made his way to the tailgate, opening it, still unable to take his eyes off of the old motorcycle. He felt like he was dreaming. He pulled a long, wooden board out of the bed, positioned it like a ramp and then scampered up next to the bike, where he began untying the straps. Once unhooked, Mr. Kelly and Frank helped him gingerly push it off of the truck.

"Okay," Mr. Kelly began, pointing to various parts of the bike, "here's where the gas goes, the oil... you've got your brake and clutch pedals... kick starter... shifter... I think that's about it, Gary."

Gary tossed the ramp back into the truck and shut the tailgate. "Okay, Mr. Kelly... thanks a lot. I promise I'll take good care of 'er."

"I know you will." Mr. Kelly smiled, putting his hand on Gary's shoulder. "You remind me a lot of Bobby when he was your age. Keep your chin up and your nose clean, and you'll have a bright future."

"Okay, Mr. Kelly... I will." Gary watched as he took one last look at the bike and then got in the truck.

"Good luck, boys!" he called. "And thank you again!"

"Bye!" Gary replied, moving to the open window. "Have fun in Florida."

Mr. Kelly laughed. "Oh, I'll have fun, alright... Don't forget your promise."

"I won't."

He started the truck and put it in gear. "So long, fellas."

Gary waved goodbye and watched as the pick-up swung around and headed for home, stirring up the dusty road.

"I'm goin' home," Frank said sullenly, turning away.

"What? Why? You're not gonna help me with this thing?"

Frank stopped. "No."

"Why?"

"Because I don't want to, that's why. You wanted it. It's yours."

"Oh, c'mon, Frankie..."

"Don't 'Frankie' me, Gary. You drag me all over the countryside, make me sleep in a barn, almost get me killed jumping onto a train, and then drag me all over the countryside *again*... All so *you* could end up getting a motorcycle. Did you even stop to think about my half of the reward? You didn't even ask me about it."

Gary felt the back of his neck heat up. "What? I didn't do all of this just to get a motorcycle! And you should'a said something! Besides, I'll let you ride it, too!"

"Oh, you will, huh? Yeah, right. What the heck are you even gonna do with a motorcycle? You can't even ride it for another *four* years! And even if I would'a said something, you wouldn't have listened, just like always!"

"What are you even-"

"I'm done," Frank interrupted, pointing at Gary. "Finished. I'm never listening to one of your stupid ideas ever again. All I ever get is either in trouble, hurt or, worst of all, nothing. Like today. You always seem to come out smellin' like a rose, and don't even care what happens to me. Well, not anymore, 'cause I ain't gonna stand for it." He spit on the ground. "Have fun pushin' your new best friend all the way home."

Gary had grown so angry that he could barely see straight. If he was completely honest, it was the truth in Frank's words that stung the most, if for no other reason than he was left with no defense. Furious and without a word, he got on the bike a began trying to kick start it. It was still a little too tall and heavy for him and he had trouble balancing it on one leg.

"Gary... what do you think you're doin'?" Frank asked wearily. "You don't know how to ride that thing..."

"Bet me, asshole," Gary spat. "Go on home to your mommy and your teddy bear and your stupid chess board. I don't need you... I don't need *any*body!" The kick starter wasn't working, so he decided to try and push start it. Walking the bike out into the middle of the road, he pulled the shifter into second gear and hopped on, pressing the clutch pedal down with one foot and pushing with the other. He hoped Frank was watching. Rolling down the gentle slope of Webber Road, he picked up speed quickly. When he thought he was going fast enough, he side-stepped the clutch pedal and the bike jerked, bucked, sputtered and finally hacked itself to life, helped along by Gary feathering the throttle. The engine roared through the four short exhaust pipes. He'd show Frank, he thought to himself, shoving the shifter into first and gunning the throttle. He wasn't expecting the bike to stand straight up and take off like a rocket, though, nor was he expecting the throttle to stick open. He tried to slow it down with the brake pedal, but when he pressed it, nothing happened. The years of storage had not been good to the bike, he suddenly realized as he bounced along, hanging on for dear life, continuing to pick up speed. He was completely out of control.

"Gary...! Gary, wake up! *Gary!*"

Gary felt himself being shaken into consciousness. And then he felt everything else. His head was throbbing, his ribs were on fire, and his right leg felt like someone had smashed into it with a cement truck. Hot pins and needles pulsed through his entire body.

"Gary!" came Frank's frantic call again, sounding muffled and distant.

He struggled to open his eyes, but his vision was nothing more than a red blur, and all he could make out was Frank's silhouette kneeling beside him. "W-what...?" he managed weakly. He could taste blood. A lot of blood.

"C'mon, Gary! Stay awake! We gotta get you to the hospital!"

Gary tried to remember where he was and why, but to no avail. The only thing he could recall was seeing a tree line rushing toward him. And then a barbed wire fence, which he soon realized was still tangled around his body.

"Don't you dare die!"

The last thing he felt was being lifted off of the ground by unsteady hands, his body hanging limp like a rag doll. The pain shot through every nerve like lightning; it was excruciating. He quickly blacked out again.

April 17th - Three days later...

"Gary?"

Grandma Kate's voice pulled Gary from his fitful slumber. He slowly open his eye, the one that wasn't swollen shut, and looked around. She stood over his hospital bed.

"Someone's here to see you, dear..." She stepped aside, revealing Frank standing in the doorway. After a quick whisper to him, she left the room.

"Boy, are you a sight..." Frank said, coming closer. "You look terrible."

"I feel terrible," Gary replied hoarsely. "The drugs they give me aren't worth a darn..."

"Well..." Frank sat on the edge of the bed. "You're lucky you're still alive."

"Yeah, I know... Thanks to you."

"How long do you gotta wear this cast?" Frank asked, tapping Gary's leg.

"I don't know. I've been too scared to ask."

Frank chuckled. "What? You? Scared?"

Gary did his best to smile. "Yeah... I guess I'm not as tough as I thought I was."

"Oh, I don't know... if you could'a seen yourself, you never would'a thought you'd live."

"Really? I was that bad?"

"Really. You broke down a whole section of barbed wire fence and got wrapped up in it. Your face, your neck, your arms and legs... I didn't even know people had that much blood."

"Wow..."

"See?" Frank said, holding up his arms for Gary to view. They were covered in hundreds of tiny, scabbing gashes.

"Wow..." Gary exclaimed softly. He felt a lump growing in his throat. "I'm sorry, Frank. I really am. For everything."

"I know you are, pal... I'm just glad I got to you quick enough."

"Gramps said you carried me all the way to your house."

"Yeah... I tried to go to Guthrie's, but nobody was home. My place was the next closest. Then Mom called the ambulance and here you are. I really didn't think you were gonna make it..."

Gary felt a few tears filling up his good eye. He realized that if it wasn't for Frank, he probably would have been laying in a casket instead of a hospital bed. And while he could never completely replace Huey, Frank was just about as good a friend as he could ever ask for.

"Thanks, Frank..."

Frank smiled. "Anytime, pal."

"You wanna sign my cast?"

"Sure."

"There's a felt pen over there," Gary said, motioning to his bedside table.

Frank scooped it up and began writing, reading out loud as he always did, "From your best pal Frankie... Until our next big, crazy adventure..."

Chapter 5
´A Nickel´s Worth´

Friday, August 3rd, 1951 - Age 12

"That was a good one, Gramps," Gary said, tossing the last few pieces of popcorn into his mouth as they descended the concrete front steps of King's Cinema, out into the warm summer air.

"I agree," Roy replied, placing his fedora back on. "But, boy, your grandmother wouldn't. Too much suspense."

Stepping onto the sidewalk, they were bathed in the rainbow glow of King's multicolored neon marquee. Gary stopped to tie his shoe. "Yeah, she only likes those musical pictures. Or romance ones. I like these thrillers." He jabbed his thumb at the marquee, which read in block letters: *'Alfred Hitchcock's 'Strangers on a Train'.* "Maybe if Frank gets back from vacation in time, I can take him to see it, too. He'd prob'ly love it."

"Oh, I'm sure this one will be around for a few more weeks, at least."

As he was attending to his shoe laces, Gary happened to glance across the street at next door's Jack's All-American. Something familiar caught his attention through the window; long, blonde, curly hair. "Hey, isn't that..." he trailed off.

"Isn't what?"

He didn't reply immediately. Instead, he stood and took a few steps closer. His initial assumption was correct; it was Candy. Sitting across from another young man, laughing. Holding his hand. Sharing a Cherry Coke float. Giving him doe eyes. Gary felt his chest instantly tighten into a ball of hurt and confusion.

"What is it, Gary?"

"That's..." He could scarcely believe it enough to say it. How could she do this to him? After two whole years? "There's Candy..."

"Where?"

"In Jack's..." He pointed. "She told me she was sick..."

"I don't see..." Roy said, following Gary's finger. He fell silent.

"Who's that kid with her?" Gary croaked. "Why is she with that kid, Gramps? Why's she holding his hand?"

Roy gripped Gary's shoulder. "Come on, son. Let's go home..."

-♠-

Gary tossed and turned. Trying to sleep was useless. He kept replaying the entire scene over and over in his mind, and the more he did, the tighter the knot in his stomach became. Occasionally, a tear would escape his eye, which only made him more angry; he was on his way to becoming a man and felt that crying about such things was a relapse into childish behavior. But he couldn't hold them back.

For hours, he rode a roller coaster of sadness, anger, hatred, confusion and, most of all, feeling betrayed. It was only then that he realized how attached he'd become to Candy. Even if he hadn't really, truly, deeply loved her, as he had confessed to Frank, he'd become accustomed to her presence in his life, and could scarcely believe that she would - or could - betray him in such a manner, after all of the time they'd spent together.

Between flashes of bitterness, he would recall moments that they had shared, such as their first kiss behind the grange hall, or going trick or treating together, when they had dressed up like Bonnie and Clyde. Images filled his mind of them riding bikes, picnicking, walking to school together, necking in the empty dugouts... simply just sharing in life's experiences. All of that seemed so pointless now, like such a waste of time.

He imagined what it would've been like to ram his grandfather's car into the side of Jack's, while she was still sitting there. That would teach her. But then he realized that she was far from worth destroying a vehicle over. In fact, he realized that now she couldn't have been worth less in his mind. In that moment, as he stared intently out his bedroom window, all sadness left him, and was quickly replaced with complete and total hatred.

-♠-

"What'd you do, wet the bed?" Roy asked, taking a sip of coffee. "You're up awfully early."

Gary, already fully dressed, stumbled to the kitchen table and pulled out a chair across from his grandfather. The clock on the wall showed that it was just a bit past six 'o clock. "No, Gramps... I didn't sleep very well." In fact, he hadn't slept at all. He rubbed his eyes vigorously. The morning sun was just beginning to peek through the open windows of the large kitchen, and birdsong filled the cool, refreshing air that wafted in.

"Could that possibly have anything to do with last night?"

Gary laid his head on the table. "...Possibly."

Roy sat his newspaper down and stood, grabbing an empty mug from the cupboard. He poured Gary some coffee. "Here."

"Thanks..."

Sitting back down, he began, "Look, Gary... I know that anything I say right now isn't going to make you feel any better. But this is all just part of growing up. You'd be very fortunate in life if this was the one and only time that you got your heart broken by a girl, believe me."

"I know... I just... I'm not even really that sad. I'm mad."

"A perfectly natural reaction, I would say. But it isn't doing you any good to *stay* mad. You're a smart young man, Gary. You know that you're not gaining any ground by wallowing in the past. You've got to get up, brush yourself off, and keep going. You have no other choice, unless you want to forfeit your future in trade for an unchangeable past. What happened last night is done. Over. Irreversible. But what happens today... well, that's a different story."

Gary let his grandfather's words of wisdom sink in for a moment. He was right, as usual. He still hated Candy, though. "How come you always know all this stuff?"

"Because, Gary, believe it or not, a very, very long time ago, I was once a young man. And I made many mistakes, but I always determined not to make the same one twice. Hanging onto your past is a mistake that will cost you more than anything else in life." He downed the last of his coffee.

"How come?"

"Because, son... it *costs* you life."

"Hmm... But why would she do this? Do you think it was 'cause of my scar?" Gary pointed to the white streak beneath his left eye, one of several keepsakes that he'd picked up during his bout with the barbed wire fence. It was something that he'd grown very self-conscious about.

"No, Gary, I doubt it."

"Then why?"

Roy shrugged. "I don't know. You may never know. Maybe *she* doesn't even know."

"Well, *she's* stupid."

"We're all entitled to make mistakes, Gary. The only thing that makes someone stupid is not learning from them."

Gary sighed. She was stupid, no matter what his grandfather said. "Well... *now* what am I supposed to do?"

"What do you *want* to do?"

There was a dangerous question, Gary thought. If he did what he wanted to do, he'd probably end up in prison. "Honestly, Gramps? I wanna get even. I wanna go out and go on dates with as many girls as possible, an' I want Candy to see every single one of 'em."

"Well, that wouldn't be very fair to all those other girls, would it? Using them as a tool to get even?"

Gary sighed again. "No... I guess not. But it'd be fun..."

"Mmm, for a while, maybe. But in the end you'd still be letting the situation control you, instead of the other way around. You'd be walking backwards through life, letting your past decide where you're going." Roy leaned closer. "You have to look at this like a blank slate, Gary, full of endless possibilities. It's an opportunity to start fresh. And that's how you should look at every so-called 'set back' that comes your way. If you do that, you'll be miles and miles ahead of everyone else, because the only thing that can change your future..." he tapped his finger on the table for emphasis, "...the *only* thing that can make a difference, is what you do right now, in this moment, today." He sat back in his chair again, letting his words hang in the air. "And everyone's heard that, but very, very few take it to heart. You should only look to your past for wisdom, never for direction. It has no idea where you even are."

"But... I don't understand..."

"How can something that's stuck behind you guide you forward?"

"I guess it can't."

"But most everyone lives that way, driving ahead while looking in the rear view mirror. In your situation, don't let what Candice *did* determine what you *do*; that would only throw you into a viscous cycle in which you'd keep recreating the same outcome. Understand now?"

Gary nodded slowly. "Yeah... I think so." He smiled a bit. "You're so smart, Gramps."

Roy smiled back, leaning forward and playfully nudging Gary's jaw with his fist. "It's in your blood, boy. You'll catch up."

Monday, August 6th, 3 days later...

The gentle whine of his bicycle's tires on the sizzling blacktop set Gary's pitch as he enthusiastically hummed out *'When Johnny Comes Marching Home'*, simultaneously trying not to drop his baseball and bat, the former of which was gripped precariously in tandem with the bat handle, and the latter of which rested on his shoulder. The afternoon sun overhead was unmercifully broiling the countryside; it felt as if it were about three inches from his face. He assumed it had to be at least a hundred degrees.

Traveling north on Webber, he continued his impromptu concert for one until, having just started the song for the fifth time, he felt something snap and his feet immediately began pedaling much faster and with much less resistance than normal. The initial jerk loosened the ball and bat from his grip and sent them skipping across the road.

"Aww... dammit," he said, dragging his feet on the ground, having lost his coaster brake. He turned off of the blacktop and into the grass. "Son of a..." One look at the bike confirmed his suspicion; a broken chain. "Great. Of all the..." he muttered to himself, walking across the road to retrieve his baseball affects before they got run over.

Making his way back, he remembered that his grandfather had shown him how to fix a broken chain, as long as all of the pieces were there. He stooped down to examine it. Sure enough, the master link was gone. "Perfect. Juuust perfect..."

He began a thorough search of the area, unwilling to even consider pushing the bike all of the way back home in the sweltering heat, and quickly found the largest half of the link, but the rest of it evaded him. He had resorted to crawling on his hands and knees, sweeping through the grassy burm, when he heard a car slow down and stop.

"Gary Bell?" came a familiar voice.

Gary stood and squinted at the sunlight gleaming off of the vehicle's chrome trim. He recognized the car and matched it with the voice. "Principal Martens?"

"What in heaven's name are you doing?"

"I was just on my way to the ball field an' my chain broke... See?" he said, holding up the piece he'd found. He watched as Martens pulled off of the road behind his bike and got out. He was dressed in casual clothes, which made him look a bit strange to Gary; he had only ever seen him in a suit and tie.

"I thought you were hurt or something... It's a little dangerous to be crawling around on the road," he said in a fatherly tone. "All kinds of crazy drivers around here... like me." He laughed.

Gary had grown to like Principal Martens. He felt understood by him, accepted, and although he wouldn't label him a 'friend', he definitely fell into the 'ally' category. "Yeah... I guess you're right. I found half of the master link, but that's all."

"Where did the chain break?"

"Right around in here," Gary replied, pointing at the ground around his feet. "I can't find the clip."

Martens began searching alongside him. "Let me see the link," he said.

Gary handed it over. "If I had a paper clip or somethin', I could fix it."

"Well, unfortunately, I don't have one. Normally I'm swimming in them, but... Hmm." He handed the link back and scanned the ground for another moment. "Tell you what, Gary... I'm just on my way into town. We can put your bike in the trunk and stop at Fleisher's. I'm sure he'd have a new one."

"It wouldn't be too much trouble?"

"Of course not. I'm going right by there."

"Well... Okay, thanks!" He began walking back to his bike, greatly relieved that he wasn't going to be pushing it home. "What are you goin' into town for?"

"Just going to look at the new house."

"New house? You're movin' to Carson Creek?"

"Yep! Living in Flintridge isn't what it used to be. Plus, I'll be closer to the school. And Mrs. Martens' family lives here, so it'll work out better for everyone."

"Well, that's great! I wouldn't wanna live in Flintridge, either..." He reached the bike and wheeled it to the back of the car. Martens opened the trunk for him. "Can I put my ball and bat back here, too?" he grunted, lifting his bike into the car.

"Certainly. I think there's enough room in here to *play* ball if you wanted to..." he said, chuckling.

Gary laughed, scooping them out of the grass and tossing them on top of his bike. Martens shut the trunk lid. Walking to the passenger door, Gary said, "Yeah, this car is one of my favorites, Mr. Martens, I think it's..." He stopped short with his hand on the door latch. Sitting in the passenger seat was one of the most adorable members of the opposite sex that he'd ever laid eyes on. "...beautiful," he finished his sentence in a mumble.

She looked up from a notebook she'd been writing in and smiled at him. "Hi," she said.

"Uhh... hi." Gary's hand instinctively jumped to cover the scar below his eye. She was dressed rather plainly; a plaid button-up shirt and blue jeans rolled to the knees, but she had a natural, unblemished beauty about her that he'd never seen in a young girl before. Her walnut-hued hair, streaked blonde by the sun, was pulled into a high ponytail, and her eyes... Gary had never seen eyes so incredibly full of... full of something so wonderful that a name had yet to be invented for it; they glistened like dark chocolate diamonds.

"Gary," Martens said, opening the driver's door, "this is my daughter Samantha... Sam, this is Mr. Gary Bell. You read about him in the paper last year, remember?"

"Hi," Samantha said again, flashing Gary another perfect smile.

"Hi..." Her smile was different; formed as much with her eyes as with her mouth, and it was so genuine, so inviting, that just the sight of it immediately warmed him from head to toe. He felt as if his feet had been cemented in place.

"Sweetheart, do you mind hopping in the backseat? We just have to run Gary into town."

"Oh, okay..." She began gathering up her notebook and pencil.

Gary forced himself to snap out of his reverie, which had begun to center around the dry, but somehow melodic, sweetness of her voice. "No. No, I can ride in the back, Mr. Martens... I'll just... ride in the... back..."

"So, Gary," Martens said, "how's your leg feeling?"

"It's fine," Gary replied quietly. He was almost embarrassed to speak, feeling that anything he said would sully the beauty that he was beholding, although Samantha was sitting sideways on the front seat with her back to the door, so he tried to reel in his urge to stare, lest he come across as anything but being in total awe.

"Gary here was in a *motorcycle* accident, Sam."

"Really?" she asked, looking back at him, her eyes growing larger than their already natural doe-ness. "A *real* motorcycle?"

"Mm-hmm." Gary nodded. He wiped the sweat from

his forehead.

"What all did you break again?" Martens asked, looking at Gary in the rear view mirror.

"Just my leg. And some ribs... And some, uhh... fingers." Every word that tumbled out of his mouth tasted like gasoline. "...And my cheekbone."

"Oh my God..." Samantha exclaimed, and then quickly covered her mouth. "Oops. Sorry, Dad..." She turned back toward Gary and mouthed 'Oh my God' again.

"It wasn't that bad... Mostly."

"Is that how you got that scar?"

Gary suddenly felt his face heat up. He bit his lip and nodded, cursing himself under his breath.

"Sam..." Mr. Martens chided.

"What? I just wondered..." She looked back at Gary and smiled apologetically. "Sorry."

"No... It's okay. I don't mind," he lied.

"It doesn't look bad or anything. It actually looks kinda... good on you. It fits you."

Gary felt something like warm honey flow down over his entire body. "Uh... thanks..."

"Samantha, I'm sure Gary doesn't want to hear you talk about his scars..."

Martens was wrong. Gary would gladly listen to her talk about anything. Scars, broken bones, diarrhea... anything. Just as long as he got to hear her voice and look at her face.

"Samantha here is going to be in the eighth grade. She's not looking forward to having her father also be her principal," Martens said, laughing. He slowed as they passed into city limits.

"It'll be better than going to Flintridge High," Samantha said, furrowing her brow. "That was going to be awful..."

Eighth grade. She was a year older than him. That

hadn't been a problem with Margret Henchy, but he hadn't really liked her anyway. He was a little disappointed.

"What grade are you going into, Gary?" she asked.

It was the first time he'd heard her say his name. It sent tingles through his brain. "Seventh. Seventh grade. I'm only twelve." An image immediately flashed through his mind of him caving his own skull in with a sledgehammer.

"Me too..." she said. "I skipped fifth."

"Ohhh..." That meant two things: one, she wasn't too old for him, and two, she was smarter than he was. He wasn't sure how he felt about that. It had definitely been the other way around with Candy; she was a bubble brain, in his humble opinion.

"Do you live here in town?" she asked.

"Uh, no. I live back that way." He poked his thumb behind him. "In the hills."

"Aww... I've always wanted to live outside of town. Away from all of the noise and bustle."

Mr. Martens braked for a stop sign. "I think you'll find Carson Creek a little more subdued than Flintridge, Sam," he said.

"I hope so," she replied, and then turned back to Gary. "Do you like it here? At Carson Valley?"

"Well..." With his principal sitting in the front seat, Gary forced himself to stretch the truth a bit. "Yeah, it's great. They have good lunches."

"And a *great* principal," Martens laughed. He pulled up to the curb in front of Fleisher's Hardware and cut the engine. "Right, Gary?"

"Yeah... for sure."

"You coming in, Sam?" Martens asked, taking the keys from the ignition.

"Sure. I've never been here before." She smiled at Gary. "I love exploring new places."

Gary staved off another shiver as he pushed open his door.

Fleisher's sat halfway down Kensington Street, taking up the first floor of a three story, red brick building that also housed a number of apartments. Its recessed front entrance was flanked on both sides by meticulously crafted window displays; an elaborate HO scale electric train scene in one, and a combination of screw drivers, wrenches, drills and various other hand tools in the other, all carefully organized according to size and shape. The interior was no less impressive; everything was neat and orderly, laid out like a fine-tuned library. Gary loved Fleisher's. As evidenced by the running train set, it was more of an amalgamation of hobby and hardware, rather than being all business, and it was always his first stop whenever he came into a little cash. But in that moment he wasn't thinking about such childish things as model boats and airplanes. He was thinking about the fact that, since they had left the car, Samantha had remained at his side, even after her father had wandered off to the paint department.

"These are so neat," she said, holding up one of the models, an old balsa wood kit of the USS Shangri-La.

"We built that one. Me and my friend Frank." He noticed that she was every bit as tall as he was, and compensated by rocking forward on his toes.

"Really? That's so neat. Can I see it sometime?"

"Uhh... actually... we blew it up." Along with his first big chance to impress her, he thought.

"You blew it up. Are you for real?" She laughed.

"Yeah. With fireworks."

"Wow... That's just crazy."

"That's what my Grandma Kate said."

"You have a Grandma Kate? My sister's name is Kate."

"Hmm. Small world." That sounded so incredibly stupid, he realized. That's not how you're supposed to use that phrase...

"She's going to get her driver's license tomorrow."

"Wow, lucky her." Gary moved from the model section to the bicycle parts. Samantha stayed right beside him. At one point her hand brushed up against his and he thought he felt his heart stop for a moment.

"So... what do you need here again?" she asked.

"Uh, a new master link. For my bike chain," he replied, crouching down in front of a wooden cabinet full of small, labeled drawers.

"What's a master link?" She settled down beside him.

"One of these," he said. He pulled the partial piece from his pocket and showed it to her. "Only I need a whole one. Careful. It's greasy."

"Ohh..." She took it in her fingers and began scanning the cabinet drawers. "Like this?" she asked, opening a drawer and pulling out exactly what he was looking for.

"Uhh... yeah, thanks."

"It's forty-five cents." She pointed to the price on the drawer.

"Oh... okay." Dammit, he thought. He stood up and stuck his hand in his pocket, coming out with a quarter and three nickels. He'd left his wallet at home, not having planned on needing it. Perhaps that's why his chain had broken in the first place; his good luck Ace of Spades card was in it.

"Looks like... you're a little short."

"Yeah... I forgot my wallet." Great. What was he going to do now?

"Here," she said, reaching into her own pocket,

pulling out a half dollar. "I'll trade you your forty cents for fifty."

"Oh, no, I couldn't... I, I mean, I can't take your money." He felt humiliated.

"Sure you can," she said. She scooped the change out of his palm and replaced it with a shiny new Franklin. "What else are you going to do?"

"Well... No, I can just walk home," he said, holding it out for her to take back.

"After coming all this way? Look," she folded his fingers closed over the coin, "if it makes you feel better, you can pay me back later, okay?"

"Well... I guess that'd be okay..." As degrading as it was, at least it would mean that he'd be guaranteed to see her again. "Thanks..."

"No problem. Is that all you needed?"

"Yeah, this is it," he said, starting for the cash register. "Where's your dad?"

"Who knows... He's probably still looking at the paint. He's so excited about this new house that he can barely stand it."

"Are you excited?"

She smiled.

Wondering why she hadn't answered him, Gary stepped up to the counter. "Hi, Larry," he said, addressing the man behind the cash register.

"Hey, how's it going, Gary?" Larry Fleisher asked, adjusting his thick glasses.

"I broke my bike chain..." He slid the master link and Samantha's half dollar across the counter.

"Oh, no. Well, that's what I'm here for, right?"

"Yep."

"Who's your friend here?" he asked, punching numbers into the cash register.

"Uh..." Gary glanced at Samantha. "This is

Samantha. She's getting ready to move here from Flintridge." He took his change from Larry.

"Well, congratulations, Samantha. Welcome. When are you moving?"

"Next week. If you see my Dad, can you tell him we went outside?"

"Why certainly, darlin'. The gentleman in the paint department?"

"Yes... Thank you!" she said, pulling Gary by the elbow.

"Uh... Bye, Larry..." Gary mumbled, allowing himself to be led by the arm.

"So long, Gary. Good luck!"

Gary turned to see Larry give him a thumbs up and an exaggerated wink. "Th-thanks..."

Gary squinted at the blazing sun as he stepped back out onto the sidewalk, with Samantha's hand still on his elbow. She led him to a bench in front of the building and sat down.

"Can you keep a secret?" she asked, looking serious.

"Uhh..." Gary was surprised by her sudden change in demeanor. "Yeah... I guess so."

"No, no 'guess so'."

"Okay. I can."

"Okay, well..." She looked around, making sure no one was in earshot. "Here goes... I'm actually really scared to death about moving to the new school, but I don't want my Dad to know."

"Why?"

"Why what?

"Why... both things."

"I'm scared because he's the principal, and I'm worried that other kids are going to... you know, not be nice. And I don't want him to know, because he's already so stressed about the whole thing..."

"He is? He doesn't seem-"

"Oh, he is. About moving, the new school year, my sisters and me transferring... all of it. And I don't want to add to that, but I'm really worried."

"Okay..." Gary wasn't quite sure what to say. Candy had never shared any of her feelings with him. "What... What do you want me to do?"

She looked at him for a moment. "Nothing. I just wanted you to know."

He was sure there was more to it than that. Maybe he should try to comfort her. "Umm, okay, well... I don't think you need to worry. Most of the kids are pretty nice, mostly."

"Really?"

Her expression softened a bit, so Gary knew that he was on the right track. "Yeah, and your dad really is a good principal. I'm sure he'll take care of you if kids do anything to you."

"But that's the thing," she said, turning serious again, "I don't want other kids thinking I'm getting special treatment. That just makes them even worse."

"Oh... How do you know?"

"My Mom is the Sunday school teacher at our church. You wouldn't *believe* how mean those kids can be."

"Really? Sunday school kids?"

"Yes. I mean, they won't beat you up or anything, but sometimes they'll say something, or do something small that just... hurts. In here." She pointed to her heart.

Gary furrowed his brow. How anyone could ever do anything to hurt a girl like Samantha was completely beyond him, and just the thought of it made his blood boil. Nothing brought him out of his shell like anger. "Well, if anyone at Carson Valley does that, you come find *me*. I don't care if it's a kindygartner or a senior, I'll bury 'em in the playground."

She laughed and looked away, smiling. "That's what I wanted to hear," she said.

"And I mean it, too. If anybody messes with you, even a little tiny bit, I'll make 'em pay, they'll be sorry they were even born. I'll kick their a-"

"Okay, okay," she interrupted, putting her hand on his arm. "I just wanted to know that I had an ally."

"Well... you do. I won't let anybody hurt you, Samantha."

She smiled again, softly. "Promise?"

"Cross my heart an' hope to die."

"What in the world is taking my dad so long?" she said suddenly, standing up. She turned and looked through Fleisher's front window. "Oh, he's paying now."

"Oh! That reminds me..." Gary said, standing up next to her. He reached into his pocket and handed her the nickel he'd gotten as change. "Here. I'll still owe you five cents."

Samantha bit her lip, thinking for a moment. And then her gaze slowly shifted from the coin to Gary. She looked him directly in the eyes, a slightly mischievous smile playing across her face. "Keep it. Buy me a Coke sometime..."

With those last five words, Gary felt as if he'd just won a million dollars and a lifetime supply of everything wonderful in the world.

Chapter 6
Romance and The Reaper

Saturday, February 14th, 1952 - Age 13

He'd finally done it. After months and months of pushing, pleading and prodding, Gary had, at long last, taken Samantha on a real date. Or at least as close as Mr. Martens would let it come to being a real date; Sam's sister, Kathryn, had been selected as their combination chauffeur and chaperon, mainly because she had already made plans to attend the Grange Hall's St. Valentine's Day dance herself, with her boyfriend Greg, who was one of the event planners. As Kathryn helmed her father's Buick

towards home through the dark, winding hills south of
Whitefeather Lake, Gary sat with his arm around Sam in
the backseat, stealing kisses when Kate wasn't looking.

Even in light of the constrictions, it had been a
wonderful evening; he'd danced with Sam for hours,
holding her as close and tight as possible, in spite of old
Mrs. Guthrie admonishing him to 'leave room for Jesus'.
Gary laughed to himself. Jesus could get his own girl. Sam
was all his.

"What's so funny?" she asked, pulling her head from
his shoulder.

"Nothin'. Just happy, that's all."

"Mmm, me too..." She suddenly sat up. "*Ooo*, turn up
the radio, Kate! I *love* this song!"

"Oh, jeeze, Sam..." Kate answered from the driver's
seat. "You guys just danced to this like five minutes ago...
And I need to concentrate on the road. I can hardly see
through all this snow..." But she raised the volume
anyway, filling the car with Johnny Ray's'Cry'.

Samantha immediately began singing along. "*...it's
no secret you'll feel better if you... crrr-ryyy...* Come on,
Gary, sing it!" she laughed.

Gary shook his head. "Oh, no. No, no... you don't
want *me* to sing."

"Oh, come on!"

"Hmm-mm. Not gonna do it. Can't. But *you* should
keep singing." He liked her voice.

"Oh, you're such a baby... Sing with me, Kate!"

"I told you, Sam; I have to concentrate. The road's
slippery, so pipe down back there..."

Gary looked out the front window. Kate was right; it
was a nearly a white-out. What had earlier been light
flurries had turned into a blowing, blinding blizzard,
almost too thick for the car's headlights to pierce. It was
caking the windshield as fast as the wipers could scrape it

away.

"I'm really glad we got to do this," Samantha said, lowering her voice.

"Me, too. I had fun," Gary replied. He tugged his tie loose. The only part he didn't like about going on dates was having to dress nice. But the flip side was that Samantha had gotten dolled up, too, and she looked especially pretty in her white satin dress and matching wool coat. He squeezed her hand. "And you were the best lookin' dame there, Sam."

She laughed. "Oh, I'm a 'dame' now, huh? What's next? You going to call me your 'moll'?"

"Say, that's not a bad idea..." Gary smiled. "I'll grab my tommy gun and getaway car when we get home."

When her laughing subsided, Sam turned and looked him in the eyes, whispering ever-so-sweetly, "I'll be your moll, Gary Bell..." She put her hand on his cheek.

Gary didn't care if Kate was watching or not; that kind of sweetness had to be tasted. He kissed her softly on the lips, feeling her hand move from his cheek to the back of his head, holding him there. The connection he felt with her in that moment went beyond what he was able process with his mind. If he died right then, he thought, he'd die the happiest young man on Earth.

"You have the prettiest eyes..." she said, pulling back slightly.

"Huh? *Pretty?*"

"Oh, jeeze... Handsome. You have the handsomest eyes, okay?"

"That's better..." He chuckled.

"They're green and blue and brown, all at the same time. I've never seen anything like it."

"Hmm. I guess I never paid that much attention to them." He pointed to his left eye. "I messed this one up when I crashed my motorcycle. See the scar in there?"

"Oh, yeah... Aww, does it hurt?"

"Only if I rub it a lot. But I can't see right out of that eye anymore. Everything's a little blurry."

"That's awful..."

"Yeah... I guess barbed wire will do that. I was pretty lucky I didn't lose it."

Sam laid her head back. "For sure. You wouldn't look nearly as handsome with an eyepatch."

"Well, I could'a got a wooden eye... Painted it white an' scared all the little kids."

"Ha! Yeah, that would've probably scared me away, too."

"And if I lost my baseball, could just pop it out an' keep playin'."

Samantha giggled. "Gary, you're just... crazy. You know that?"

"I've heard that a time or two, yeah."

"But I like it... And I like you. A lot."

"Well, that's quite a coincidence... I like me a lot, too."

She playfully punched him in the ribs. "I'm serious!"

"Oww... So am I!"

"Smart aleck... I don't have time for such childishness," she said, with an air of mock disgust.

"That so, huh? Well I think you should make-" He was cut off by a cry coming from the front seat. The car lurched.

"Ohhh... Ohh, *no!*"

He jumped forward in his seat to see Kathryn fighting the steering wheel, jerking it left and right. She had come over a steep hill and run directly onto a sheet of solid ice.

"Slow down, Kate!" Sam yelled, gripping the back of her sister's seat.

"I'm trying, I'm trying! The brakes are locked up!"

They were sliding sideways down the incline, picking up speed. Gary tried to think, tried to keep calm amidst Kate's yelling, but then, through a break in the snow, he caught a glimpse of what laid directly ahead of them. The blood drained from his face. "Holy shit..."

"What? What?" Samantha exclaimed.

"Hang on!" he yelled, grabbing her, wrapping his arms around her tight. "Keep your head down!"

"*Why?* What's happening?!"

Before Gary could answer, the road curved off to the left, and sent them sailing across the deep ditch at the bottom of the hill. For a split second everything went silent. Then the passenger side tires slammed into the opposite bank, violently flipping them over onto the roof. They began to barrel roll. Gary held onto Sam as best as he could; they were being tumbled all over the back seat and ceiling like clothes in the dryer. The windows broke out. Glass filled the air around them. Metal squealed and snapped. He squeezed his eyes shut as tight as they would go, desperately wishing that this nightmare would stop, and then, finally, the car slammed down on its roof one last time and began sliding. It eventually slowed to a heaving stop, and everything went silent. Nothing but a few falling glass shards and the sound of the radio still playing.

"Are y-you okay?" Samantha asked, her voice full of fear.

"We need to get out of here," Gary replied sternly. "Now."

"Kate? *Kate!* Gary, she's...!"

Kathryn was laying on the overturned ceiling in front of them, in a heap, not moving.

"Samantha, just get out *now!*" He began pushing her toward one of the blown out windows.

"But-"

"I'll get her, you need to go!"

"Why?" she yelled back, through her sprouting tears.

As if to answer her, a loud, baritone *'crack'* came from below, followed by a slow, steady crunching sound.

"Because," Gary replied with all of the calmness that he could muster, "we're sitting in the middle of Pike's Pond."

A look of complete terror dawned on her face. "Oh... my God..."

"Go!"

She began scampering for the window on her hands and knees, but it was too late; with one final, deafening *'crunch!'* the ice gave way, instantly plunging them into the freezing, black abyss below.

The icy water, rushing in through the broken windows, immediately rose up to Gary's chest. "Sam!" he yelled, unable to see in the pitch darkness. He could hear her whimpering in the shrinking space.

"I-I'm right here!" her voice echoed.

He reached out until he found her. Grabbing her by the arm, he pulled her closer.

"Gary," she wept, "are we going to die?"

"No, Samantha. We're gettin' outta here. We're gonna swim to the surface." As soon as he said it, he remembered that he didn't know how to swim. He felt the car settle on the pond floor.

"Kate! Where's Kate?"

Gary forced himself to think. Every second was precious. "Sam. You're gonna have to go by yourself. I'll get Kate."

"I don't think I can-"

"You don't have any choice. Go now. Take a deep breath."

Through her crying, Samantha inhaled deeply.

"I'll be right behind you," Gary said, and then he put

his hand on her head and pushed her under the freezing water, guiding her toward and out of the back window. No time to waste. He took a deep breath of his own and plunged under, feeling his way to the front. The water was so frigid on his face that he nearly gasped beneath the surface. His hand passed over the dome light. He was close. A few inches more and he bumped into Kathryn's unmoving form. He grabbed onto her coat and began pulling her backward. Please don't be dead, Kate, he thought to himself. He reached the rear window and pulled her through, passing beneath the trunk deck and out into the open water. Now for the hard part. Kicking off of the bottom, he tried to lift her up, but she was too heavy; her thick, full-length wool coat was anchoring them in place. He tried to pull it off, but quickly realized that it was buttoned from the top to the bottom. Okay, keep calm. Stay focused. Don't panic. Working only by touch, he popped the buttons loose one by one. The coat fluttered open. He peeled it off of her and kicked at the pond floor again, and this time they slowly began rising.

He tried his best to follow the path of the bubbles escaping from the car below, in order to surface where the ice had broken. He pumped his legs as hard as he could. His lungs were burning. They began to fight against him, rapidly expanding and contracting, desperate for oxygen. A faint light rippled on the surface above. Exerting himself as he was, he couldn't hold his breath any longer; his lungs exploded, expelling all of their spent oxygen out into the water in a flurry of bubbles. He started to panic. He wasn't ready to die. Unable to stop himself, he began to inhale, sucking in the freezing pond water, but just as he started to cough, mercifully, they broke the surface and he immediately vomited it all out, gasping frantically for fresh air. He grabbed the edge of the ice break and pushed Kate out of the water, coughing uncontrollably. He had done it. Pulling himself up with his elbows onto the slippery wet ice next to Kate, he nearly collapsed.

"Sam!" he yelled hoarsely through his gasps.

No reply.

He lifted his head. She was nowhere in sight. At first, he thought perhaps she had run to get help, but then he heard a very faint tapping sound coming from his left. He froze. She was trapped beneath the ice. "Oh, God... no..." Without thinking, he dove back in.

Samantha was about ten feet away from the hole; Gary could barely make out her white dress gently floating in the water. Doing his best not to sink like a rock, he pumped his numb arms and legs frantically in her direction. He hoped against hope that he wasn't too late. Due to his inexperience as a swimmer, it seemed like it took him forever to reach her. When he finally did, he grabbed her around the waist and began pulling her back toward the break with all of the speed and strength he could conjure up. A moment later, he broke the surface again and nearly threw Samantha out onto the ice.

She began gasping and coughing just as he had.

Gary pulled himself out for a second time. Sam was alive. He had to get to Kate. Rolling her over on her back, he could see that she wasn't breathing, and even in the dim light her bare arms, legs and face appeared pale and bluish. A large gash crossed her forehead. "Kate!" he yelled, shaking her. "Kathryn!" She didn't respond. Not know what else to do, he pressed his fists into her stomach. Water ran out of her mouth and nose. He did it a second time with the same result. "Wake up!"

Sam, shivering uncontrollably, feebly crawled over next to him, bawling. "Kate? Kate!"

Gary continued to pump out the pond water until, miraculously, she began coughing, followed by deep, frantic breaths. She immediately began convulsing; upon waking up, her body began going into shock. Her eyes opened wide.

"Kathryn!" Sam yelled again, scooting over to cradle her sister's head in her lap.

A tsunami of relief washed over Gary's quivering body. It was only then that he realized how cold he was; his white cotton shirt had been soaked translucent, and his dress pants clung to his legs like plastic wrap. He knew that he had to get them help fast, before hypothermia sat in. He began to stand. His legs felt like wet noodles. "Sam?" he said through chattering teeth, trying to keep his feet beneath him on the slippery ice, "I'm gonna go get help. Try and pull her off the ice and then stay here, okay?"

"O-okay. Hurry." She looked up at him, body racked with violent shivers, her tear-filled eyes pleading. "P-please hur-ry..."

"Do what you can to warm her up. I'll be back..."

Gary stumbled out onto the road and began running, fueled by pure adrenaline. Katherine's life was in his hands. Maybe Samantha's, too. He had no time to think about his burning face and hands, or the fact that every other part of his body was completely numb. He could barely even feel his feet slapping against the icy pavement. Through the blizzard, the lights of Carson Creek flickered about a mile to the south. He silently prayed that he would make it in time.

"Right up here! See the tracks?" Gary exclaimed, pointing through the front windshield.

"I see 'em... Good *Lord*..." The driver said quietly.

Gary hadn't even gotten the man's name. He'd burst unannounced into the first house he'd come to and interrupted a family card game. After quickly explaining the situation to him, the man had phoned the authorities and rushed out to his sedan, with Gary on his heels.

"There's a couple'a blankets in the back," the man said, skidding to a stop. "Grab 'em."

Gary did as he was told and then jumped from the vehicle, quickly catching and surpassing the man. He leapt over the ditch and made his way back down to the pond. There, huddled together near the shore, sat Sam and Kathryn. "Sam!" he called.

"We're over here!" She was still crying.

Gary slid to a stop in front of them and quickly threw one of the blankets around Kate's shoulders. She was sitting up, leaning against Samantha and staring blankly into the snow, quivering. "Kathryn! Are you okay...?"

She shifted her gaze to him. "Y-yes... I'm... I'll be alright..."

The man caught up with them. "Here," he said, grabbing Kathryn and heaving her up into his arms, "let's get you girls to the car. To the heat." He began trudging through the snow back toward the road.

"Can you get up?" Gary asked Samantha, wrapping the second blanket around her.

"I-I think so..." She began to stand, bare legs shaking.

"The ambulance is on the way." He finished helping her to her feet and started guiding her toward the car. "We're gonna be okay, Sam... We're gonna be okay."

Samantha looked up at him, her eyes blurry with tears. "Thank you, Gary..." She leaned into him. Throwing half of the heavy blanket around him, she laid her head on his shoulder, completely exhausted. "...Thank you..."

Gary pulled her close as they shuffled through the foot-deep snow, leaving their would-be grave behind. He managed a weary grin. "How's that for a first date?"

Sam looked up at him again and laughed weakly through her tears. "Oh, Gary..." She sniffled. "Just remind me to bring my swimsuit next time..."

Chapter 7
The Ghost of Nathaniel Brighton

Friday, November 28th, 1952 - Age 13

The sweet aroma of burning leaves permeated the countryside as Gary, Samantha and Frank cut across one of Grandpa Roy's many rolling fields, heading east toward the hills. The air was unseasonably mild, and the crystal clear sapphire sky was the perfect backdrop for the many Canadian Geese still flying south for the winter, piercing the wild blue yonder with their traditional 'V' formations. It was warm enough that Gary had stripped off his jacket, opting to hang it over his shoulder and make the trek in just a sweater.

"How far is it?" Samantha asked, reaching out and

grabbing his hand.

"Oh, only about a hundred more miles."

"Alright, smarty pants... How far is it, Frank?"

Frank was busy scanning the barren field for arrowheads, running across its dry, dusty surface with a large stick he'd found."Huh? Oh, it's just in back of those trees over there..." He pointed to the hills without looking up.

"Frank," Gary said,"the best time to find arrowheads is right after they plow. This stuff still has the-"

"Ah-ha! Found one!" Frank exclaimed, scooping the piece of flint out of the soil. "What was that you were sayin', Gary?"

"I *said*... when are you gonna tell us who your new girlfriend is?"

"Yeah, Frank," Sam said, "who is she anyway?"

Gary put his arm around Samantha. She had become an integral part of their little crew over the summer, joining in all manner of expeditions and adventures in which she had proved her ability to keep up with - and sometimes surpass - he and Frank. The last several months, however, her time had begun to be swallowed up more and more by an increasing amount of schoolwork and home responsibilities. Today was a treat for Gary, being that it was the day after Thanksgiving and they were all home from school.

"Ohh... You guys'll find out soon enough who she is..." Frank said, sounding mischievous.

Sam rolled her eyes. "Well, at least tell us her name."

"Nope. That'd be too easy."

"Her initials, then." Gary said.

"Hmm..." Frank paused for a moment. "Okay... L.T."

Gary began laughing. "I knew it! Looney Toon!"

"Very funny, smartass. No, that's not her name."

Samantha appeared to be deep in thought, and then a

lightbulb came on. "Lisa Thomassina," she said, very matter-of-factly. "You're going steady with Lisa Thomassina."

Frank frowned, turning his attention back to the ground. "You guys are no fun at all."

"Oh my gosh," Gary exclaimed. "That's her? I should'a known you'd be goin' out with a tuba player!"

"Hey... What's *that* supposed to mean?"

"Uh, nothin'. How come she's not here with you now? She could'a come along."

"Because. She doesn't like you."

"Good." Samantha said.

"Doesn't like me? Who doesn't like *me?*"

"Well... Lisa, obviously."

"But... why?"

"Does it matter?" Sam asked, elbowing Gary in the ribs.

"She thinks you're wild and reckless. And a bad influence."

"Oww... Where in the *world* would she ever get an idea like that?"

"Mmm, I don't know... Maybe that time you called the fire department from school so you could skip that Friday afternoon test. Or maybe it was when you stole all of the 'for sale' signs around town and put them in the school's front yard... but those are just guesses."

"So I don't like school... It's not like I'm a serial killer or somethin'."

"Sorry, pal. I tried to tell her what an angel you are, but she just wouldn't listen."

"Well... You can tell her that I don't like *her*, either."

"I'll let 'er know... Say, look at this..." Frank crouched down and picked up what appeared to be a tiny, gold ring. "Who's your grandpa got renting these fields? Elves?" He laughed, holding it up.

"That looks like a baby ring..." Samantha said, taking it from Frank.

"How fitting," Gary quipped.

"Oh, Gary... I had one just like this when I was a baby." She took a closer look, wiping away the dirt. "Wow... It's twenty-four karat gold."

"Really?" Frank exclaimed. "You can tell just by lookin' at it?"

"Yeah. It says so on the inside."

"Well, hot dog! I feel like a regular treasure hunter!"

"It's probably cursed," Gary said, laughing.

"Yeah," Frank nodded, retrieving it from Sam, "that *would* be my luck..."

They reached the edge of the field and began high-stepping through the bordering barricade of bushes, brambles and thistles, all of which had long since lost their greenery. Soon they made it to the barren trees at the foot of Eastlake Ridge's southernmost tip.

"There," Gary put his hand on Samantha's shoulder and pointed, "through the trees..."

"I don't... Oh! Wow, it's just sitting there?"

"Yep. For about the last twenty years."

The closer they got, the easier it became to identify; an old abandoned house nestled among the decaying foliage. It was massive. A colonial-style with a wrap-around porch, it looked like every haunted house that Gary had ever seen; peeling paint, broken windows, missing siding and a large hole in the roof were just a few of its maladies.

"You guys have been here before?" Sam asked.

"Oh, yeah," Frank replied. "We even slept in it on Halloween this year. Until about nine-thirty."

"In the morning?"

"No. Nine-thirty at night."

"What happened?"

Frank fell silent.

"Go ahead. Tell 'er Frank," Gary prodded. "Tell 'er why we left."

Frank frowned. "You were scared, too, I know you were."

"Right... Keep tellin' yourself that."

"Wow..." Samantha marveled as they stepped onto what at one time had been the front yard. She turned to Gary, holding his hand with both of hers and saying excitedly, "I wish we could try staying here again... That would be so neat!"

"Yeah, I don't think your dad's gonna let you spend the night with me, Sam. No matter how grateful he is."

"Oh, he wouldn't have to know... I could come up with something." She looked back toward the house. "I'll bet it was beautiful... Who left it here?"

"Gramps said that some guy and his family lived here a long time ago. He lost everything in the Depression and went crazy and shot himself, right there in that attic window. It's haunted."

"Oh, bull puckey..."

"Samantha!" Frank exclaimed. "Lady language!"

Sam ignored him. "Can we go inside?"

"Yeah, c'mon," Gary replied, pulling her forward. "It ain't bad during the day."

Opening the heavy front door took a bit of persuasion, coming in the form of Gary's boot. "Been awhile..." he said as it swung inward, nearly tearing the hinges from the rotten doorframe. They stepped inside.

"Wow..." Samantha said, pushing away a crop of cobwebs hanging from the high ceiling.

"Watch your step." Gary motioned to the floor. More than a few of the boards were missing. "Frank an' me took some of those to build our tree house."

"Who needs a tree house when you can have a *real* house?" Sam asked. "Look at this! There are even still paintings on the wall!"

"I know. It's like the people just... vanished."

"Check this out, Sam," Frank said, waving her over to a door in the wall. He opened it. "Simple closet, right?"

"Yeah... Looks like it..."

"Wrong." He stooped down and located a tiny hole in the floor and pulled upward. It swung open, revealing a small, hidden compartment.

"Neat... What's that for?"

"Near as we can figure," Gary answered, "they hid stuff in there."

Samantha laughed. "Oh, really? I never would've guessed."

Frank shut the floor. "There's all kinda weird stuff like that in this place."

"Yeah," Gary said, "we spent days here looking for hidden money or treasure or other valuable stuff, until we realized that if this guy had anything like that he prob'ly wouldn't have shot himself... Here, Sam, you like to read..." He led her into an adjacent room, the library, where the walls were lined with dusty bookshelves still packed with thousands of books. Large, mostly shattered windows to the left filled the room with light.

"Oh my gosh..." she exclaimed quietly.

"If you want any, take 'em. I'm never gonna use them."

"But... I can't just *take* them, can I?"

"Sure. Gramps owns this place. Take whatever you want," he said, walking to a wooden chair. He sat down and pulled out a cigarette.

Samantha began running her fingers over the cobwebbed spines. "This is so amazing..."

"I knew you'd like it."

"Gary," Frank said, sitting on the floor, "did you ever ask your grandpa about that old jeep out at the hangar?"

"Yeah, he said it belongs to some guy in Cherry Hill."

"Hmm. That stinks."

"But that doesn't mean we can't take it for a little spin sometime..."

"Oh, wow!" Samantha said, pulling something from the shelves. "Look at this, guys!"

"What?"

She held up an old, thick, leather bound book. "It's a photo album!" Blowing off several decades worth of dust, she walked to Gary and sat down on his knee, opening it.

"Neat-o..." Frank scooted closer.

"Gosh, pictures..." Gary said, putting his hand on Samantha's bottom as nonchalantly as possible, trying to make it seem like he was steadying her.

"Stop it..." she said, squirming slightly. "Look at this... 'Brighton Family Photos'..."

"Yeah, I think I remember Gramps saying that was their names." Gary pointed to one of the photos. "Look; there's this house."

"Oh, my... It *was* beautiful... That must be them standing in the front yard."

"Tough lookin' fella." Frank said.

"Yeah, he looks like Burt Lancaster..." Gary replied.

Samantha turned the page. "Look how pretty the wife was. And their children..." She continued to flip through the album, pointing out bits that interested her.

"Hey, wait a minute, Sam," Gary said, leaning forward. "Turn back a page."

"What?"

"Frank, look at this..." Gary pointed to a photo of Mrs. Brighton sitting in the backyard with her children.

"What about it?"

"Look at the house there... There's a basement entrance. I don't ever remember seeing that."

"Well, I'll be... And I don't ever remember seeing anything like an exit *in* the basement... do you?"

Gary looked at Frank. "You know what that means, don't you?"

Sam cut in, saying excitedly, "It means there's a part of the basement that you guys haven't explored yet!"

Gary smiled, nodding. "Not for long..."

Rounding the corner of the house, Gary soon realized why they'd never noticed the entrance; apart from the heavy cover of weeds and brambles, the earth had been mounded up against the rear of the house, completely covering the the horizontal doors. "There... It's right there under that window..."

They set to work clearing the area with sticks, rocks and an old, rusty ax that Frank had found in the small shed off to the right side of the yard. After about thirty minutes, their tools began hitting something solid.

"This is so exciting!" Samantha said, trying to wipe a dirt smudge from her cheek.

"I wonder why he would'a hid this..." Frank panted. "Guy *must'a* been crazy... Maybe there's dead bodies inside!"

"Look," Gary said, "there's one of the handles... Ah, shit. There's a lock."

Frank tapped the soft wood with the ax. "I don't think we gotta worry about the lock... Feels like we could break a hole right through this door."

They continued to excavate until the entrance was

completely uncovered, and then Gary stood, mopping his brow. "Okay, stand back," he said, taking the ax from Frank. He swung it high over his head and brought it down with a loud *'crack!'*, instantly splintering the rotten wood.

"Atta boy!" Frank said.

Gary swung a few more times until he had made a hole large enough to peer through. He got down on his knees and stuck his lighter through, flicking it to life.

"What do you see?" Sam asked.

"Nothing... it's still too dark. Whew. Stinks in there, though." He stood again and took a swing at the lock. The latch broke away from the door. "There we go... Now we're in business!" Frank helped him tug the double doors open.

"So exciting!" Samantha said, stepping forward.

Gary put his hand on her shoulder. "Hang on, wait a minute."

"What?"

"I don't want you gettin' hurt... I'll go first." He glanced down into the cellar. A flight of rickety-looking wooden steps led into the darkness.

"Good idea," Frank said. "That looks... pretty creepy."

Gary gingerly placed a foot on the top step, testing its integrity. It creaked softly, but seemed sturdy enough. He began descending into the cellar. "Sure wish we had a flashlight," he said, re-igniting his Zippo.

"See anything?" Sam called. "Can I come down?"

Gary stepped off onto the dirt floor. The air was stale and musty. "Yeah, come on. I don't see anything. It just looks like an old fruit cellar to me." The lighter flickered over walls lined with shelves, laden down with dozens and dozens of now unidentifiable canned goods.

"Wow..." Sam said, coming down the stairs with

Frank in tow. "This place is..."

"Disgusting," Frank said, picking up one of the jars. Its contents had evolved into something that resembled lumpy black tar. "Do you think this could be a... an internal body part? Ooo, gross!"

Sam paid him no mind. "I wonder how long it's been since somebody was down here..."

"Well," Gary replied, "at the very least it's been twenty years. Looks like it flooded at some point..."

They continued to scour the room for several minutes until Frank exclaimed, "Hey! Looky here!" He pushed aside some jars and pulled out a rusty metal lock box about the size of a cinder block. "Whatcha think this is, Gary? It's heavy!"

"Is it locked?"

"Uh... yeah."

"Come on, bring it outside!" Gary said, quickly ascending the steps and snatching up the ax "Here, put it on the ground." With a precisely-placed swing, he made short work of the small lock. He got down on his knees and slowly began opening the lid, and then stopped. He took a deep breath, trying not to show too much excitement.

"What?" Samantha asked. "Why are you stopping? Open it!"

"But what if it's nothing? What if-"

"Oh my Lord," Sam said, grabbing the lid and throwing it back.

All three of them gasped in unison. Cash. Silver. Gold. Important-looking papers. The box was completely packed.

"Holy..." Gary exclaimed.

"...Christ." Frank finished.

Samantha carefully pulled out a five hundred dollar bill. "Oh my... *goodness*. How much do you think is here?"

"More than I've ever seen in one place..."

"We're rich, Gary!" Frank said, grabbing a handful of bills and jumping up. "We're *rich!*"

Gary shook his head, laughing. "I know! I-I can't believe it!"

"Wait a minute, wait a minute," Samantha said. "Look... There's a letter." She tugged at an envelope that had been taped to the inside of the lid and opened it, pulling out a single page, handwritten note.

"What's it say?" Gary asked, unable to take his eyes off of their treasure.

Samantha began reading, "It says, 'To my dearest Bridgette... If you are reading this, I have failed in my attempt to reason with or overpower Mister's Goti and Novello, and very likely have passed on into the next life. But, thankfully, you have succeeded in deciphering my clue to finding this box. They are coming here today to collect what I owe them, which is why I have sent you away with young William and Violet, to keep you safe from their vile, monstrous clutches. They are evil men, overseen by men eviler still. I have not enough to pay them and they will not be satisfied until they have taken what they wish. Going to the authorities would only postpone their wrath, and possibly place you and the children in jeopardy. The valuables enclosed in this safe are all that remains of my family's fortune, and you must use it to begin life anew. I love you, my dear, and the children, too. I regret that I have not more time to write, but I must hide this box before their arrival. I fear that I have already looked upon your face for the last time, my love, but it will be the whole of my final memory.'..." Samantha sniffed. "It's signed, 'Always and forever yours, Nathaniel'."

A sober silence descended upon them.

"I guess he wasn't crazy after all..." Gary finally said, softly.

"Yeah..." Frank replied. "Must've had the Mob after him or somethin'..."

Samantha wiped away her tears. She looked at the box and then to Gary. "We can't keep this, Gary."

He nodded slowly, coming to that realization himself. As much as he hated to admit it, this small fortune definitely belonged to someone else. And he was going to see that they got it.

Tuesday, December 2nd - 4 days later...

"Well," Roy said, turning off the truck, "I guess this is the place."

"Looks a little run-down," Gary replied. "You sure someone still lives here?"

"According to Lieutenant Rigby. You want me to come along?"

Gary's eyes roamed over the dilapidated, single story home, just one in a long line of similar abodes. It was just a step up from a shack; sections of the roof had been patched with tin, parts of the siding had fallen off, and chickens crowded the wire-fenced front lawn like inmates, a dozen or so cats taking on the role of prison guards. "No... I'll go, Gramps. If I start screamin', then you should come in." He opened the door and stepped out into the cold, taking the metal box and photo album with him, the latter of which Samantha had insisted he bring along.

Walking past the mailbox, he noticed the name 'B. Brighton' painted on its side. This was the place, alright. With Sam busy at home and Frank having evening band practice, it was up to him to be the ambassador for their little trio. As he unlatched the gate, he heard the front door open.

"Can I help you, young man?" a woman's voice called from behind the screen. "I'm not buying anything."

Gary shut the gate behind him and walked up the uneven sidewalk. "Mrs. Brighton?"

"Yes, that's me. Who are you?"

When he got closer, Gary immediately recognized her as the woman from the photo album, albeit several decades older and looking a bit worse for wear. "My name is Gary Bell."

"Well, Gary Bell... I'll ask again; can I help you?"

"Maybe, Ma'am," Gary said, stepping onto the front porch. "I think I have something you might want to see."

"You're not going to try and sell me something, are you?" she asked warily.

"No, Ma'am."

"Well..." She slowly opened the door, glancing at the metal box. "Come in, then."

"Thank you." Gary stepped inside, wiping his feet on the rug. The interior of the house was no more spectacular than the outside, but it was relatively clean and neat. Cats and kittens darted about as he entered the living room behind Mrs. Brighton. She was in her mid-forties, slender, with graying auburn hair and tired, blue, crow's foot-bordered eyes. She wore a simple green cotton dress.

"Now, young man..." Her speech was crisp and clear, spoken like someone of class, but it also carried a tinge of weariness. "What is this all about?"

Gary produced the photo album from beneath his arm and handed it to her. "I think this belongs to you..."

Mrs. Brighton's brow furrowed as she warily took the album. All confusion disappeared as soon as she opened it. "Oh, my..." she said, her voice wavering. Tears filled her eyes as she settled into a chair and began flipping through the pages. "How did you know...?"

"My grandfather owns your old house. Me and my friends found that there. Well, actually, my girl found the album..." He sat the box at her feet. "And we found this, too."

Mrs. Brighton's confusion returned. "What's this?"

Gary pulled the handwritten letter from his coat pocket and handed it to her. "This will explain everything. Do you mind if I sit down?"

"Of course not, dear," she said, opening the envelope. "Please, sit."

Gary did so, settling into a small couch across from her. He was immediately pounced upon by a tiny, tortoise shell kitten.

"Oh, don't mind the cats," Mrs. Brighton said, pulling the note out, "they're about to run me out of house and..." She fell silent when she realized what she was holding.

Trying to protect his fingers from the playful feline's teeth, Gary watched Mrs. Brighton's eyes slowly scan down the letter. He wondered how she could even read through all her tears as she reached the end. He turned his attention to the kitten, not wanting to stare. It soon settled down and began letting him pet her.

Mrs. Brighton tried to say something through her sobbing, but it just came out as a gasp. Forcing herself to take deep breaths, she reached down and opened the box. Her weeping resumed two-fold. "Forgive me," she managed.

"No, no... It's alright." Gary continued to appease the wild beast sitting on his lap while Mrs. Brighton slowly regained her composure.

"I apologize, darling," she sniffled. "And thank you. You have absolutely no idea how much..." She held up the letter, shaking her head, fighting back another wave of tears. "Everyone thought he'd... he'd taken his own life. After that, everything fell apart, but now..." She looked down at the box. "I am in complete shock. I can't thank you enough."

"Well, I did have help. They couldn't be here." Gary had promised Samantha and Frank that he'd give them equal credit, which they deserved. "We're from Carson Creek."

"Oh, so far away, too... You must extend my many thanks to your friends."

"I will, ma'am." He looked down and smiled. The kitten was now purring up a storm, kneading his leg as fast as her tiny paws would go. She looked as contented as could be. Strangely, it made him miss Huey.

Mrs. Brighton sighed. "Oh, where are my manners? May I offer you some water?"

"No, no thank you, ma'am. My Grandpa's waiting outside. He wants to get home before it gets too dark."

She gently folded the letter and slipped it back into its envelope. "I feel so indebted to you," she said, placing it in the photo album, still shaking her head in disbelief. "I wish there was something that I could do for you..."

Gary remembered the fiasco he'd gotten himself into after returning Mr. Kelly's puppy. They had agreed on no rewards this time. "No, ma'am. I'm- we're just happy to have helped."

"Do you and your friends like pumpkin pie?"

He wasn't sure about Sam and Frank, but he *hated* even the *smell* of pumpkin pie, passionately, and wasn't about to ride all of the way home with one. "No, that's okay, Mrs. Brighton. Thank you."

"Oh, darling, but there must be something..."

"What in the world...?" Grandpa Roy exclaimed as

Gary got back in the truck.

Gary waved goodbye to Mrs. Brighton through the window, still seeing tears glistening in her eyes. She waved back. He was genuinely happy to have helped her, and as much as he would've enjoyed spending his cut of the cash, he knew that they had done the right thing. She needed it far worse than he did.

"What in the world?" Roy said again. "What's *that?*"

Gary turned to his grandfather. "What? Oh, this? This is Charlie. She's a girl." He pulled back his coat to reveal the little multicolored kitten nestled inside. Before Roy could protest, he added, "She wasn't a reward, Gramps. I paid twenty-five cents for her. Mrs. Brighton just asked if I'd take care of her for a little while. She said she had too many to give enough attention to them all."

"Hmm... A 'little while', huh?"

"Yeah. Just a little while."

"I'm going to assume that your 'little while' and my 'little while' are going to mean two completely different things in this case."

Gary smiled, looking down at his new furry friend. She mewed at him, rubbing her head against his chest. "Yeah... You're prob'ly right..."

Chapter 8
'Cowboys and Hula Girls'

Tuesday, May 26th, 1953 - Age 14

"*Get it off! Get it off'a me!*" Gary screamed, writhing futilely against the agony engulfing him.

He loved working at A&L Automotive. Having been his summer job the previous year, thanks to his grandfather's acquaintance with co-owner Jack LaRue, he was all set to spend another three months expanding his knowledge of the ins and outs of vehicle mechanics, beyond the simple oil changes and brake jobs that he'd learned to perform the year before. Cars fascinated him. Maybe even more so than girls. Ever since he was eight years old, when he'd spotted Crane McCall's hot rod jalopy barreling out of the school parking lot, engine screaming and rear tires squalling, he was hooked.

With school letting out in three days, he'd decided to get a head start on the job, just to get himself reacquainted with Mr. LaRue and his partner 'Ace' Axemberg, and the old white repair shop at the corner of Webber and Main. And though he hadn't been thrilled about his first assignment that evening being a run-of-the-mill oil change, it was something other than farm work. It wasn't until the vehicle he was working on rolled backward down the ramps and onto his arm that he wished he was still at home gathering eggs.

"Help!" he called again, pulling against the weight of the sedan, trying to roll it backward. It was no use. Warm, slick oil poured down on him from the open oil pan drain, preventing him from getting a grip on the underside of the car. Tears of pain welled up in his eyes.

A moment later, Ace, a gruff-looking thirty-something with prominently graying temples, shot through the office door at the far end of the shop. "What the hell, Gary?" he exclaimed, skidding to a stop beside the car.

"It's on my arm!"

Cursing and grunting, Ace grabbed the vehicle and pushed it backward.

Gary rolled unto his side, clutching his right arm tightly against his chest as the pain began to mount. "Shhh..." he hissed.

"Are you hurt bad?" Ace asked, reaching down to help Gary up.

"Yeah..." Gary answered through gritted teeth. "I can't feel my fingers..."

"Shit... Come on. Let's getcha to the doctor..."

Saturday, May 30th
Annual School's End Jr. High/High School Costume Ball

"Oh, you look *fine*..." Samantha said, walking arm-in-arm with Gary toward the high school gymnasium.

"Yeah, right. It looks like I was trying to dress up like Popeye and quit halfway through..." He looked down at his right arm. The cast created an inhuman bulge beneath his western-style, long sleeved shirt, resembling a plaid-wrapped tree limb from the elbow down. He couldn't even button the cuff. "It's terrible."

Sam sighed. "No it isn't... I'm sure even cowboys broke their arms sometimes."

"Yeah, well..." He adjusted his Stetson hat. "...not *this* cowboy."

"You look fine," she said again.

"I don't know why we even have to..." Gary trailed off, deciding against arguing over their attendance of the costume ball for the umpteenth time. He hated such social events, and if it hadn't been for Samantha's incessant begging and pleading, he'd be at home, happily listening to the Indians game. The dance had been a source of contention between them for the past several months, but she had finally won out. Even fracturing his arm wasn't a good enough excuse to skip it. Before he could dig another hole for himself, he said, "*You're* the one who looks fine... I can't believe your pop let you out of the house like that."

Samantha looked down at her hula girl costume, complete with lei, flowing grass skirt and coconut bra. A large white flower had been tucked behind her ear. "Why? It's cultural."

"Cultural..." Gary snorted. "You're gonna dance around barefoot all night?"

"Gary, I am completely dedicated to this charade," she said, laughing.

"Good. 'Cause you ain't gettin' my cowboy boots."

"I *'ain't'?*"

"You *are not* getting my boots... that better?" He said, rolling his eyes.

Sam playfully nudged him with her elbow. "I'm just trying to get you to sound respectable... and I don't want your stinky old boots, anyway."

"Good. I'm not carryin' you around all night, either."

"Oh, I'll be fine... And *you'll* be fine, too. Lighten up. You have to have some *fun* sometimes, grumpy..."

They reached the gymnasium entrance and Gary opened the door for her. "I do. It just always seems to involve the exact opposite of what we're doing..."

"Hey!" Frank yelled as Gary and Samantha entered the large, brightly decorated gym. "Roy Rogers made it!" He was made up to resemble an ancient Egyptian mummy, wrapped in yards and yards of white cotton fabric, with only his eyes showing.

"Hopalong Cassidy," Gary said flatly. "I don't think mummies wore glasses, Frank."

Frank shrugged, laughing. "They do now!" He looked at Samantha. "Say... that's quite a getup, there, Sam..."

"Why, thank you, Franklin..." she said, ruffling her grass skirt. "Where's Lisa?"

"Oh, she's over there with a bunch'a spacemen... I was just gonna get us some punch. You guys want some?"

"Only if it bites me back," Gary replied, unsuccessfully trying to scratch beneath his cast.

Frank shook his head. "Sorry, pal. Mr. Greene's been watching the punch bowl like a hawk. There will be no spiked beverages tonight."

Gary patted his leather vest pocket. "That's what you think."

Samantha gasped. "Gary, you didn't."

"What? I gotta survive this somehow."

Frank shook his mummy-bandaged head again. "So sad. Only fourteen and he's already a lush."

"Yeah, right... Go get your punch, Cleopatra."

"Alright, don't say I never offered you anything." He turned and lumbered away through the crowd, arms outstretched, walking like Frankenstein.

"I can't believe you," Samantha said, looking perturbed. "Bringing liquor to a school dance..."

"Oh, come on, Sam. It's not the first time an' it prob'ly won't be the last. You'd better get used to it. And that's not even the worst of it." He patted the old revolver hanging from his hip. "Looks pretty genuine, don't it?"

"You've got to be kidding me... Gary you can't-"

"Oh, relax. It ain't - *it's not* - even loaded." He forced a smile and grabbed her by the hand. "C'mon. It's a slow song. Let's dance."

Parting a sea of gangsters, princesses, soldiers and football players, Gary led Sam to the center of the gym floor and took her by the waist. He felt like a robot swinging his stiff arm around. Sighing, he said, "The decorations look nice."

"They should," Sam replied. "It took us all day yesterday." They swayed in silence for a while and then she said, "Thank you, Gary. This means a lot to me. I know you think it's stupid, but..." She kissed him on the cheek. "It means a lot."

"No problem, Sam..." Gary felt like an ass. Samantha was nothing but good to him and he had to struggle not to run off and leave her on the dance floor. Not because he didn't enjoy being with her; he loved being with her, but he hated these types of social gatherings. Or *any* type of social gathering for that matter. He realized that sooner or later he was more than likely going to have to deal with the public in large quantities, but the thought made his skin crawl. He felt so out of place, so vulnerable. The cast on his arm only multiplied those feelings. Closing his eyes tight, he determined to make it through the night for Samantha, and Samantha alone.

"Are you still going to work at the garage this summer?" she asked, brushing several strands of Charlie's fur off of his shoulder.

"Yeah. As much as I can, anyway. Kinda hard to do some of that stuff with a bum arm... God, it itches..." It felt like bugs were crawling around under the cast, making him squirm involuntarily.

"How long is it on for?"

"Five to six weeks, the doctor said. Too long."

"Hmm. So how many broken bones does that make now?"

"I dunno. I lost count."

Samantha put her head on his shoulder. "You're just *so* reckless... You worry me sometimes. But then I realize... maybe that's what I like so much about you."

"Really?"

"Yeah. Everyone should be a little more reckless. It keeps life interesting."

"Ha. And painful. Besides, it's not my fault that car popped outta gear. I was just doin' my job."

"I know... It's like that type of stuff just follows you around."

"Maybe I'm just bad luck."

"Oh... Stop. You're not bad luck for me."

"The night is young, Sam. Gimme a chance."

She laughed softly. "A reckless pessimist. *There's* a new character for my book."

"Hey, now... don't be writin' stories about me unless I'm the dashing young hero that everyone loves, with a fast car, tons of cash and lotsa beautiful women... And no emotional stuff, either."

"Well..." she said, smiling, "at least you got the 'young' part right..."

Gary rolled his eyes dramatically. "Gee, thanks. Now I'm not the hero..."

A look of seriousness crossed over Samantha's face as she bit her lip, thinking. She brushed aside a straying lock of hair and glanced up at him. "You *know* you're my hero, Gary, and... and I *do* love you..."

There they were. The three words that Gary had been dreading since they'd begun going steady. And he'd laid his own trap, to boot. His grandmother was the only person he could ever recall telling him 'I love you', and even that made him incredibly uncomfortable, for reasons he couldn't fully explain or understand. He forced another smile, knowing full well that she was expecting him to return her affectionate words. But he couldn't. His throat locked up. Instead of telling her how he really, truly felt, instead of telling her that she was the most wonderful, beautiful, lovely thing that had ever happened into his life, he coughed. He didn't even cover his mouth. "Sorry," he said quickly, glancing away.

Disappointment filled Samantha's face for a moment, and then she smiled politely, as if to a stranger. "It's okay," she said, looking away herself.

The song ended and a more lively, fast paced number began in its place. Gary let go of her. "I think I'm gonna go get some of that punch," he said. "You want some?"

"No, thank you. I think I'm just going to stay here and dance for a while..."

You are, without a *doubt*, the world's *biggest* idiot, Gary thought to himself. A goddamn *fool*. He watched from the shadows, sitting in the fold down, theater-style seats, as Samantha danced by herself in the middle of the gym floor, surrounded by dozens of other happy-looking couples. Even from thirty feet away, he could tell that her smile was only for show. He'd known her long enough to see that she was heartbroken.

For a moment, he imagined himself rushing over to her, gazing deeply into her dark brown eyes, kissing her and telling her that he really did love her, over and over again. But he knew he couldn't bring himself to do that. He wasn't even sure if he knew what love really was, aside from that which he'd felt for Huey and, now, Charlie. He slid down in his seat, resting his boots on the railing in front of him. What a train wreck.

"Hey, there, cowboy..." came a soft voice from behind him.

He turned to see, of all people, Candy walking down the steps toward him. Great, he thought. Here was Satan, come to tempt him in his moment of weakness. She had opted for an angel costume, of all things. He remained silent.

"Whatcha doin' up here?"

He resisted the urge to stand up and kick her the rest of the way down the stairs. "What do you want, Candice?"

"Oh, nothing. I just saw you up here all by yourself, and... thought I'd come say hi."

"Yeah, well... Hi. So long."

"Where's your date?" she asked, coming closer. She pulled down the seat next to him and sat.

Gary shifted uncomfortably. They had only spoken a handful of times since he'd caught her cheating on him, and those talks had been anything but cordial. She was impossible to reason with. The more he thought about it, the more he wondered if sitting next to the real Satan wouldn't be more enjoyable. "She's dancing." He pulled the brim of his hat down.

"Oh, that's right... You only like to dance to slow songs."

"Yeah."

"How's your arm?"

"Fine."

"Fine? Jim Boyd told me you got hit by a car and broke it..."

"Fractured. Not broke. And I didn't get 'hit' by a car."

"Oh... What happened then?" She leaned forward and lifted his hat a little.

He jerked his head away. "Don't... touch me. Shouldn't you be out there dancing with someone?"

"Shouldn't you?"

He thought for a moment. "Listen, Candice. Samantha is ten times better than you *ever* were to me. And I wouldn't trade *one* of her for a hundred of *you*, you got it?"

"I can see she hasn't helped at all with your math..."

"Look. Here's Samantha," he lifted his hand above his head, "and here's you. Allll the way down on the ground. Underneath the ground, even. You're nothin' but a lowlife, backstabbin', scum suckin' *maggot* compared to her..." He took a deep breath and exhaled loudly, trying to corral his flaring temper.

Candy's lower lip quivered slightly. "Well, if that's really the case... how come you aren't down there with her right now?"

"Because, I-" Gary stopped short. "I don't hafta tell *you* anything. Make like a drum and beat it, will ya? Go ruin someone else's night."

Without another word, Candy stood up and began walking away, but before she reached the end of the row she turned and said, "What'd she do? Tell you she loved you or something? Boy, is she in for a ride..."

The evening continued to drag on. After a four song set of slow, romantic music, Gary's head was about to explode from all of the thoughts and emotions swirling around inside him. Did he love Samantha or didn't he? That was the million dollar question. It was easy enough to *say* he did, but did he really love her for who she was or just for how she made him feel? He'd known from the beginning that Candy fell into the latter category; he'd never even considered telling her that he loved her. Dating her had almost been like a game, like make believe. Was it *still* just a game to him, like Cowboys and Indians? Or, in this case, Hula Girls? It was all so incredibly confusing.

"I love that song," Sam said as the music died down.

"Hey, you wanna get some fresh air, Samantha?" Gary asked. "It's gettin' kinda stuffy in here."

She adjusted his shirt collar. "Sure, Gary..."

"Great... I'm about to die in here," he said, grabbing her hand.

He led her through the crowd to the back door exit, stepping out into the fresh, cool air. The sky had grown dim since they'd arrived. Stars flecked the heavens like tiny diamonds trapped in a sea of navy blue silk. Gary took a deep breath. "Ahh... That's better."

"You want to go sit somewhere?" Sam asked.

"Yeah, c'mon. I know a good spot."

"I'm cold," Samantha said, running her hands up and down her bare, goosebumped arms.

Gary had led them to the deserted baseball diamond bleachers. "Here..." he said, putting his good arm around her, pulling her close. "I'd be cold, too, if I was half naked."

"Yeah, well... I guess I'm not as clever as I thought I was."

"Sure you are. It's perfectly normal for clever people to have no common sense." He poked her in the ribs, trying to keep the tension in the air at bay.

She smiled. "Oww... Stop it..." When she stopped giggling, her smile quickly faded. "Gary, you never tell me anything."

"Huh?" Oh, great, he thought. Here we go.

"Like... When we're together I feel like the conversation is completely one-sided. You don't ever share anything."

"Okay..."

"Tell me something I don't know. Anything."

"You mean right now?"

"No, next week... *yes*, right now."

"Umm... Okay... Oh, did you know that last month Mickey Mantle hit a 565 foot home-"

"Gary, I mean about *you*," she interrupted. "Tell me something about *you*. After all this time, I still feel like I barely know you."

"Oh... well... What do you want to know?"

She sighed. "I don't know... Like, what makes you so... distant with people?"

"What are you talkin' about? I'm right here."

"Don't play dumb, Gary."

He thought for a moment. She was asking him to pull his own teeth and she didn't even know it. He drew a cigarette out of his vest pocket. "I don't think I'm distant, Sam... more like... careful."

"Okay... Okay, careful. Why?"

He shrugged, striking a match on his cast. "I dunno. Why are you *not* careful?"

"I don't know... I'm just not."

"Well, there's your answer. I just *am*." He puffed the Camel to life and waved out the match. "I don't know why, either."

"Don't you trust me?"

"What kinda question is that? Of course I trust you. I wouldn't be sitting next to you if I didn't, would I?"

She sighed again. "Never mind... We're not even on the same page."

"I don't even think we're reading the same book..."

"We're not even reading, Gary; we're writing. You and me, together. We're writing out our lives one page, one sentence, one word at a time. We're writing 'us'..."

That sounded confusing. He decided to take another crack at answering her question. "Look, Samantha... I think you're a great girl. A *really* great girl. You're one of my favorite people in the whole wide world and I'd never want you to think otherwise. You're cute, you're fun, you're... good at spelling... Of course I trust you. You're one of the few people around that I actually *do* trust."

"But you won't trust me with your heart, Gary. You don't trust me enough to love me, or at least to tell me you do."

Gary threw his hands up. "I don't even know what love *is*, Sam! I don't even know what it means!"

Samantha fell silent for a moment, and then turned to him with moistening eyes. "I'd show you if you'd let me..."

Gary silently began screaming curse words at himself. "Come on, Sam... Please don't start cryin'..."

"All I know is this: I love *you*, Gary Bell. Since the day I met you, and until the day I die... I love you."

He struggled with his inner self. He didn't know how to reply honestly. "Well... all *I* know is this: that... that if I loved *any*one at all...anyone... it'd probably... it'd probably be you." He hoped that satisfied her, almost as much as he hoped it was true; he knew he didn't want to hurt her by leading her on. "I... I *probably* love you, Samantha." He wiped the sweat from his forehead.

Samantha was silent, staring at the ground.

"Okay?" he prodded. "I'm sorry if that isn't-"

"Oh, Gary," she said, sitting up and smiling through her tears, "you don't know what hearing even just that means to me... Thank you so much..." She kissed him passionately, pushing back his cowboy hat and crawling onto his lap. She had him pinned against the bleachers for what seemed like minutes.

"Mmm-mmokay... Okay," Gary said, pulling away slightly, trying to catch his breath. He had to slow things down before they got out of hand. "Let's just... let's just..."

"Will you say it again?" she said, breathing deeply in his ear. "I just want to hear it one more time..."

Her voice being so close made his head tingle. "What...? That I probably...?"

"Yes, Gary. Say it for me... please..." She leaned over him, grabbing his shirt collar.

Gary gulped. He'd never seen her like this before. It was almost a little frightening. But just one good look into those deep, dark, sparkling eyes, brimming with affection for him, was all that it took to finally realize that he really, truly *did* love her... probably.

Chapter 9

'Stormy Hearts'

Saturday, October 3rd, 1953 - Age 14

The cold, stinging rain was blowing in sideways with such ferocity that Gary found it difficult to even open his eyes, let alone keep his umbrella from repeatedly popping inside out. The massive trees surrounding McDermott and Trask Funeral Home were being whipped around like saplings in the unceasing deluge. His coat was soaked. Dead leaves swarmed all about him.

"You comin', Gar?" Frank yelled through the wind, looking over his shoulder. He was sharing an equally uncooperative umbrella with his mother, Lilly.

"Yeah... I'm comin'." Helluva day for a funeral, he thought. Apparently Mother Nature was just as upset as he was.

The pews inside were packed end to end with mourners young and old. Mrs. Hawkins led Gary and Frank, now stripped of their soaked jackets, to several of the few remaining empty seats near the back of the room, where Gary settled in next to Frank, sighing. He immediately began having flashbacks of his mother's funeral; it was the last and only one he'd ever attended, nearly a decade earlier. He remembered feeling completely and utterly helpless, as heartbroken as a newly-turned six-year-old could be, and thinking that, perhaps by some miracle, his mother would reawaken at the last moment and run to him with open arms, scooping him up and in the process erasing the horrible nightmare that had engulfed him. But, of course, she hadn't, and as he sat next to his grief-stricken father, who had been called home early from the war, he watched as the lid was slowly, unapologetically closed on everything he'd ever known to be loving and secure. From that point forward, his life took on all of the characteristics of a poorly set bone; an aching, misaligned, permanent reminder of something fractured.

"Want some Wrigley's?" Frank asked, holding out a stick of gum.

Gary shook his head, as much to clear out the memories he was reliving as to decline Frank's offer. He turned his attention to the front of the room, where an elderly gentleman dressed in black was stepping up to the podium. The organ softly faded into silence.

"Dear friends," the man began, his voice echoing of off the walls, "we are gathered here today to honor the life of loyalty, of courage, and of sacrifice... of young Mr. Daniel Royce."

Gary had promised himself that he wouldn't cry, not in front of Frank and Mrs. Hawkins. When he'd received word that Zeus had been shot and killed by a rogue North Korean while he was preparing to return to the States, well after the Armistice, he had nearly dropped the telephone. Of all the people he had encountered in his life, Zeus had stood out to him as a shining example of bravery and self-sacrifice, an exemplary citizen, and he didn't understand why someone so valuable to the human race had been fated to die so far from his home, on the barren, godforsaken soil of communist North Korea.

Lost in his thoughts, the memorial service passed by quickly, and Gary soon found himself soaked again and sliding into the backseat of Mrs. Hawkins' sedan. Listening to the waves of rain pounding the roof as he and Frank waited for her to exit the funeral home, he caught himself somewhat resenting the fact that, due to the nature of his wounds, Zeus had been cremated, robbing Gary the opportunity of a more satisfying farewell, but word had it that his ashes were to be cast into Whitefeather Lake, which was as fitting a place as could ever be found, in his opinion. He knew that he would never again pass by its shores without thinking of Zeus, or the lessons he taught.

"I can't believe he's really gone," came Frank's voice from the front seat. His back was turned to Gary, but it sounded like he was crying.

"I know, pal..." Gary replied quietly. "I only knew him for two weeks, and I can't believe it, either... Just doesn't seem right."

Frank nodded. "I've known... I *knew* Zeus since I was six years old. Every summer he was my camp counselor.

Every summer he taught me something new... He was like a big brother... One of the... best people I've..."

Gary saw Frank bow his head and begin weeping, no longer able to hide it. He reached forward and put his hand on his friend's shoulder in an attempt to comfort him. A tear escaped his own eye.

"Sorry," Frank blubbered.

"Don't sweat it, buddy..." Gary replied, sniffing. "Tears were made for this kinda stuff."

They sat in silence for a few moments, and then Frank took a deep breath and said, "I just don't understand life, Gary... let alone dyin'. What's the point of anything? Why does everybody gotta die? Like that rabbit Mom ran over on the way up here... what'd *he* do to deserve to die, let alone Zeus?"

Gary sat back in his seat, crossing his arms and gazing out the rain-streaked window at the angry, howling, tumultuous storm outside. It was a mirror image of his soul. "I don't know, Frank... I don't have any answers anymore..."

Tuesday, October 6th - Three days later...

"Gary...?" Samantha whispered, sticking her head out of her first-story bedroom window. She rubbed the sleep from her eyes. "What's wrong?"

Gary crouched down in the bushes and held his finger up to his mouth, quieting her. "C'mon. Let's go for a walk."

"What? What time is it?" She glanced up at the cloudy night sky.

"I don't know. C'mon."

"Gary... I can't just... we have school in the morning. And... and I'm in my nightgown."

"I don't care. Just a short walk."

Samantha sighed and looked over her shoulder. "Okay... let me grab my robe." She disappeared back into her dark bedroom.

Gary glanced around, hoping that no one was awake and watching him, which, thanks to the streetlamp in front of the Martens' modest home, in direct view of Sam's bedroom, would have been easy to do. He pulled his jacket collar up.

"Here," Samantha whispered, reappearing at the window. She handed Gary a pair of flat-soled shoes.

"Alright, c'mon. I'll help you..." He reached up and grabbed her around the waist, lifting her down to the ground.

She slipped on the shoes. "What is this all-"

"This way," Gary interrupted, taking her by the hand. He led her across the back yard and through the wooden gate that stood between a row of hedges at the rear of the property, careful to open and shut it as quietly as possible. They stepped out onto a deserted, shadowy Kitson Avenue and Gary turned east. After several hundred yards they crossed the bridge over the train tracks and out of view of any would-be watchmen.

"Okay," Samantha said, breaking the silence, "what's this all about?"

Gary glanced back at her. She looked beautiful, as always, with her now slightly disheveled hair and flowing white nightgown. "I just wanted to go for a walk."

"In the middle of the night, Gary? What's wrong?"

"Nothing," he lied. "Nothing's wrong." Zeus' sudden and seemingly pointless passing had thrown him into a downward spiral of confusion-fueled, anger-driven reckless abandon that had begun to be perpetuated not only by his old friend's death, but by every painful thing he could ever recall having happened to him. Part of him hoped that Samantha could pull him out of the plunge. The other part wanted her to join him.

"Then why weren't you at school today? I mean yesterday?"

He shrugged, kicking a stone out of his path. "I don't know. Just didn't feel like it." In truth, he had spent the whole day joy riding in his grandfather's pickup truck, aimlessly roaming the entire county with a bottle of Old Harper as his copilot. Roy and Kate had yet to return from their trip to New York and their absence only fed the flames of his wayward actions.

"Just didn't feel like it, huh?"

"Nope."

She stepped up beside him and grabbed his hand. "Gary, tell me what's wrong. I tried to telephone you today, but you didn't answer. Is it about your camp counselor?"

"Can't I just go for a walk without someone constantly asking me what's wrong?" Gary shot back. "And he wasn't just a 'camp counselor', Samantha... he was one of the best people I've ever met, and now he's in a coffee can somewhere 'cause some goddamn, slant-eyed, communist *shit spawn* shot him in the back of the head. Blew his goddamn face right out. Is that something I'm just supposed to let roll off my back? Is that something I should just forgive and forget? Worthless piece'a commie shit..."

Samantha released his hand and fell silent, pulling her robe tighter around her body.

Gary sighed. He'd revealed too much. "I'm sorry, Sam... I just... I just..."

She waited for him to finish, but when he didn't, she said softly, "It's okay to be upset, Gary. I understand."

"This is... I'm *beyond* upset, Samantha... I'd like to find that little bastard and skin him alive, for real. Peel all his skin off with a dull knife and my bare hands and then roll him around in rock salt, set him on fire, and crucify him. *After* I carve out his..." he trailed off, not finishing for fear that Samantha would turn around and run back home to call the mental hospital.

"Wow... I can tell that you've given this some thought..."

"Yeah... a *lot* of thought." He resumed kicking stones, in an attempt to calm himself down. He felt Samantha slowly put her arm around him.

"What can I do, Gary? How can I help?" She laid her head on his shoulder.

He took a deep breath, shaking his head. "Damn it, Sam... Why do you always gotta be so sweet?"

"Because I love you. Even in spite of yourself." She looked up at him and smiled.

Gary thought he caught a tiny tinge of fear in her eyes. What was he doing to her, he wondered? "I'm sorry, Samantha... I'm sorry I got mad." He pulled her close and kissed her on the forehead.

"It's okay, sweetheart. I get mad, too, sometimes. It happens."

"I know, I just... I didn't mean to take it out on you... Forgive me?"

She squeezed him. "Of course..."

They soon found themselves on the outskirts of town, walking the winding, leaf-littered dirt line of Shepler Road that snaked beneath the tall oaks, maples and wild cherry trees that blanketed the rolling hills and valleys surrounding Carson Creek. The night was dark and the air brisk. Their breaths came out in small clouds that wafted gently in the slight breeze.

Samantha pulled her robe collar up over her ears. "Brrr... It's cold out here."

"Here," Gary said, stripping off his coat and handing it to her, "take this."

"No, that's alright. You're going to catch cold."

"I'll be fine. Take it."

Reluctantly, she draped the jacket over her shoulders. "Don't forget... We have to walk all the way back."

"I know... I just needed some fresh air. I needed to clear my head."

Samantha was silent for a moment, and then said, "You know, Gary, you can tell me anything, anytime. If something is bothering you, I'm here... I'm always here for you. To talk, to listen... whatever you need."

Gary crossed his arms. "I know, Sam... Thanks." He looked up from the dirt road and froze.

"You don't ever have to feel like you're..." Seeing his expression, she stopped. "What's wrong?"

Gary's eyes were fixed on an old, rusty, lopsided mailbox with the fading numbers '330' still visible on its dented side, standing at the end of a long lane bordered by tall, unruly pine trees. A dam-full of memories broke loose in his mind.

"Gary, you look like you've seen a ghost..."

With no reply, he took a few steps closer to the lane, peering around the pines until the house came into view; a large, gray, abandoned farmhouse nestled among a half dozen oak trees at the bottom of a gentle hill. It *was* a ghost; a ghost of his innocence. Though he often passed by with his grandfather, he hadn't stepped foot on the property for years, and hadn't been inside the house since the day his mother died. His father, upon returning from the Pacific, had been so broken-hearted over the ordeal that he couldn't even look at the place, let alone move back in, so Gary had remained with his grandparents. Now the house was calling to him. As if pulled by some unseen force, he began walking toward it.

"Gary...?"

The old house loomed over his head, almost in a taunting manner, daring him to step inside. Everything was as he remembered it, though now in an advanced state of disrepair, from the rose bushes his mother had planted in the flower bed to the milk can that had always sat next to the front door. He glanced over his shoulder at Samantha, who stood at the bottom of the porch steps with her arms folded tight against her stomach. Even in the darkness, she looked worried.

"Who's house is this?" she asked.

He turned his attention back to the front door. "It's nobody's..."

"Then why are we here?"

Gary didn't answer. He stepped up to the door. Hesitantly, as if he were about to touch something that had the potential to burn him, he placed his hand on the knob and turned it. The door swung open effortlessly, creaking slightly. The first thing that hit him was the aroma of citrus fruit, which still clung stubbornly to the stale air after nearly a decade of abandonment. His mother was constantly scrubbing the house from top to bottom with lemon cleaner, at least once a day, sometimes two or three times depending on how depressed she happened to be. Gary pulled out his Zippo. In its flickering light, he could see that the dust-caked furniture in the living room was still arranged exactly the way it had been on that fateful winter day, complete with what remained of the old Christmas tree, now nothing more than a withered skeleton of twigs and tinsel. He stepped inside.

"Gary, what are you doing? We need to head back..."

Through the double doorway to his left, he could see that an empty bottle of scotch and an overflowing ashtray still sat on the dining room table. The entire house seemed to have been frozen in time. Fighting the knot in his stomach, his eyes wandered to the stairway. He knew where he needed to go. "Wait here," he said. "I'll be back."

With the lighter's glow dancing on the walls, he forced himself to push open the bathroom door, staving off the urge to turn around and run out of the house. He had to face his fear. He had to face his past. If Grandpa Roy was right, then this place had him trapped, holding him back like the sticky strands of a giant spider's web. His heart began pounding as the jumpy yellow glow washed over the small bathroom, coming to rest on the bathtub. The beginning and the end, he thought. A simple porcelain tub. Where everything awful started and everything good had abandoned him. Tears filled his eyes as he knelt down in front of it. Bloodstains, long since turned brown, still streaked the white sides like a horrible, ghastly signature. The straight razor still sat on the window sill. A glass tumbler still sat on the floor in front of him.

Voices filled his head of schoolmates taunting him, calling his mother a whore and a crazy woman, voices of the older kids who had told him that she'd willingly prostituted herself to men young and old, before he had even known what that meant. He could even hear his five-year-old self calling for her to wake up, and then collapsing in the barn that night, utterly confused and heart-broken, wailing himself into a fitful sleep with Huey at his side.

He wished he could make it all disappear from his memory, start over fresh with no recollection of anything before his sixth birthday. He wished he had a giant eraser to wipe the slate clean. With tears flowing freely and without reserve, he decided that there was no better time or place to do what he could to put the past, both good and bad, where it belonged. He took one last look around the bathroom and wiped his eyes clear.

"We need to go! *Now!*" Gary yelled, bursting out of the front door.

Startled, Samantha said, "What? Why? What's-"

He grabbed her hand as he sprinted past, interrupting her questions. "Come on!" They needed to get as far away as fast as possible, before someone spotted them.

"Gary! What's going on?"

He didn't hear her. He couldn't hear anything but the sound of his feet slapping against the dirt lane and the blood pounding through his ears. As they neared the road, he allowed a quick glance over his shoulder back toward the house. Flames were already beginning to lick behind the windows.

"I... I..." Samantha stuttered, leaning against a tree while trying to catch her breath, "I can't believe you did that!"

Gary, doubled over with his hands on his knees, began laughing. He felt so much lighter, so much more alive. Adrenalin coursed through his body.

"Why are you laughing, Gary? This is serious! You just set someone's house on fire!" She pointed to the smoke rising from behind the trees on the next hill over.

"Relax, Sam... Just relax."

"No, no this time you've gone too-"

Gary put his hand on her shoulder, cutting her off. "I

said relax... It was *my* house, Samantha."

"What?"

"I owned it."

"What?" She looked completely confused. "*You* owned it?"

"Yeah. My name's on the deed." He plopped down on the ground and let out a sigh of relief. He felt as if a huge weight had been lifted from his back.

Samantha sat down beside him. "Okay... But... But *why* in the *world* would you set it on fire? That's still a crime!"

"Oh, well," he said, shrugging. "Guess I just went crazy for a minute. It happens."

"You're... You... I..." Samantha struggled to find words. "I don't even know what to say or feel right now! That was completely insane! Gary, what's wrong with... what's making you do these things? This isn't you!"

"It *is* me." He pointed to the smoke. "You have *no* idea what happened to me in that house..."

"That's because you won't tell me! Gary, if you'd just talk about things... If you'd just... I... I *want* to help you, but you won't let me!"

"What's talking with you about my problems gonna do? How's that gonna help me? All it'll do is show you parts of me you don't wanna know about... Trust me."

"How would you know? You've never even tried! It's bound to be more constructive than burning a *house* down! After all this time, you *still* won't even give me a chance! You won't even *try* to trust me!"

Gary put his arm around her, trying to calm her down. "Look. Samantha. All you need to know is that I needed to get rid of some parts of my past. I feel better now."

She bit her quivering lip and looked away, shaking her head. "For how long?"

"For... I don't know... There's nothing wrong now. I'm fine. There wasn't anything you could have-"

She stood abruptly. Looking down at him, she said, "I want to go home."

Gary sighed. He just couldn't win. "Fine..." He slowly began standing.

"No, you just stay here. I can find my own way." She slid his jacket off of her shoulders and handed it to him.

He stopped. "What?"

She was desperately trying to cling to her composure. "I'm sorry... I-I've tried to... to... You just set a *house* on fire... You scare me, Gary."

"No, wait, wait," he said, standing. He put his arms around her, feeling every bit like the jackass that he knew he was. How could he have put her through that? "Samantha, I'd never do anything to hurt you... Never. You don't ever have to be afraid of me doing anything to you."

She pulled away and looked up at him. "I'm not just afraid of what you do, Gary... I'm afraid of what you don't do."

"Well... I... You don't have to be afraid at all." He kissed her, pulling her back into his embrace. "I... I'm supposed to be here for *you*... I'm supposed to help and protect *you*, not the other way around..." After a moment, he felt her begin to cry.

"But... I wanted to... to..." Weeping openly, she pulled back from him again and began walking away. "I'm sorry, Gary... I need some time to think this over..."

"But... Sam. Think about what? What's there to think about?"

She sniffed and turned back for a moment. "Us. I love you, Gary... Maybe too much. I'm sorry... Goodnight." With that, she slowly disappeared over the hillside, her face buried in her hands.

Gary stood with his arms hanging limply at his sides,

stunned, frozen in place. What had he done? What had just happened? "But, wait..." he said quietly, "I love you, Samantha..." But she was already gone.

Chapter 10
King Crane

Saturday, June 26th, 1954 - Age 15

"What can I do for you, Gary?" The congested, gravelly-voiced Jack LaRue asked as Gary swung in through the jingling front door of A&L Auto. Jack snuffed out a cigarette in an ashtray sitting on the counter.

"Hi, Mr. LaRue," Gary said, plopping down in front of him on one of the swivel stools. "I think I need a new clutch disc for a jeep... A '42 Willys."

"Hmm..." Jack furrowed his brow. "Prob'ly won't be able to get you one 'till Tuesday at the earliest." He pulled out a phonebook-sized parts catalog and began flipping through it.

"Tuesday? Rats..." He scratched his head. If his grandfather found out that he and Frank had been joy-riding in the old jeep out at the hangar, peeling the tires up and down the runway, he'd be in deep trouble. He sighed. "Well... Okay. I don't have any other choice, I guess. How much is it gonna cost?"

Jack ran his finger across the page he'd stopped at. "It's $12.95."

"What?" Gary exclaimed. "Thirteen bucks for a little ol' clutch disc? Jeeze..." He was going to have to skip his date with Jane Rockwell that night, or at least take her somewhere that didn't cost him anything. "Okay... Call it in."

"First thing Monday morning. Remind me when you get here."

Just then Gary heard a loud rumble coming through the wall from the shop area. "What's that?" he asked.

"McCall's here getting some work done."

"Crane McCall? With his hot rod?"

Jack lit another cigarette and nodded.

"Oh, boy!" Gary said, sprinting past Jack and through the door behind the counter, bursting into the shop. There, sitting in bay two between a pair of relatively pedestrian-looking vehicles, sat Crane McCall's blood red, 1923 Ford T-bucket roadster, with Crane himself leaning over the exposed engine, working the throttle into a cacophonous frenzy. Ace was helping him, and a small group of young onlookers had gathered around; Jack's son Toby LaRue, someone who had every bit as much of a passion for fast cars as Gary did, Eddie Vinson, whom he hadn't seen much of since summer camp, Dean Krindle, a young kid who he had talked to at school several times and who seemed to be fairly bright concerning cars and engines despite his young age, and, finally, a bespectacled, greasy-haired young man named Cal Rillings, whom he didn't know, but had heard that he was building quite a reputation for himself for being a reckless showboat.

"Gary!" Ace yelled over the engine, looking up from his work. "I thought this was your day off."

"It is. I was just gettin' some stuff... What are you guys doin'?" He leaned over the grill, peering down on the spit-shined, chrome-accented engine. It looked beautiful. It *sounded* beautiful.

'King' Crane McCall looked over his shoulder at Gary. He was a well-known, tough-looking, rough and tumble hot rodder from Cherry Hill who dressed exclusively in a leather jacket and jeans, no matter what the weather or occasion was, and had a crown tattooed on the back of his neck. He had been one of Gary's heroes since childhood. "Gettin' 'er ready for the big race, kid," he said, reaching over the windshield and turning the key off. He spoke in a slow, hoarse voice that seemed to magnify his worldly-wise persona.

"Big race?" Gary asked. "Where?"

"Blossom County Dragway. You know the old airstrip north'a Willagrove?"

"Yeah..."

"They built a drag strip there, see? Tomorrow's the grand openin'. E'ry hot rodder this side'a China is gonna be there."

"Oh, yeah... I heard about that..." It sounded like heaven on earth to Gary. "So... what are you doin' to get ready?"

Ace wiped his greasy hands on a shop rag. "She's got a miss in her for some reason... Can't find out why. Just put in new plugs, new wires, new points... Ran great for awhile and now all the sudden she starts missing."

"Hmm..." Gary thought for a moment. "You check

the jets?"

"Yup," Crane replied, nodding. "An' the timin' is spot-on."

Something caught Gary's attention. "There's your problem."

"Where?"

"Number three plug wire's up against the header. Looks like it's melted pretty bad."

Crane crouched down to examine Gary's finding. "Well, I'll be damned... I think he's right, Ace."

"I knew we kept you around here for a reason, Gary," Ace said. "Hang on. I'll go get another plug wire, King."

Crane stood and placed his hands on his hips. "Good call. What's your name, kid?"

"Gary. Gary Bell."

"Oh, yeah... I heard'a you... You work here?"

"Just during the summer, mostly." Crane McCall had heard of him. That made him feel extra special.

Toby LaRue piped up, saying, "We call him 'The Lone Wolf'..."

"Oh, yeah? Cool..."

"Cool?" Eddie Vinson said. "What's that mean?"

Crane rolled his eyes. "It means good, see? Neat-o. Keen. Get the picture?"

"Oh..."

Ace returned with another spark plug wire and handed it to Crane. "Here. Let's test Gary's theory."

Crane quickly swapped out the melted one and turned the key. The hot rod fired up and purred like a mountain lion. "Think that did it!" he yelled, revving the engine. He turned to Gary. "Go for a ride?"

Gary had to stop and ask himself if he'd heard Crane correctly. "A ride? You bet I do!"

"Well, c'mon. Hop on in." Crane jumped over the door and into the driver's seat, putting on his sunglasses.

"Back in a flash, Ace."

Gary could scarcely believe his luck as he walked around and slid in next to Crane. His excitement was barely containable.

"Alright," Crane said, throwing the tall shifter into reverse, "let's make us some noise..." He backed out of the garage and, after a few quick revs, pulled out onto Webber Road, turning left.

The old t-bucket rumbled through the residential part of town at a reasonable pace, but as soon as they had passed by the city limit sign, Crane downshifted and stomped on the gas pedal, squalling the tires and throwing Gary backward in his seat. Exhilarated, his eyes danced from the sun-drenched road to the speedometer, which quickly climbed to and past 80 miles per hour. Then past 100. The acceleration increased the pressure against Gary's chest like a vice, taking his breath away.

"Yeah!" Crane yelled over the deafening combination of open exhaust and roof. "She's a ready teddy, now, kid!"

The roaring wind whipped through Gary's hair and made his eyes water, which was just as well; it covered up his otherwise embarrassing tears of joy. He had never felt anything like it in his life. He was hooked.

"What happened to going to the movies?" Jane Rockwell asked, hooking her arm around Gary's as they strolled down the brightly lit Main Street sidewalk. She was tall and slender, just the way Gary liked his women, and that evening she had opted to wear a sophisticated-looking black skirt and white blouse, which, in his humble opinion, accentuated her in all of the right places. Jane was his third girlfriend since Samantha had left him, preceded by Veronica Rokissian and Judy Halladay, both of whom had proved to be far less enjoyable company than Sam. The verdict was still out on Jane. He liked her a lot; she was easy going, always ready for a date, and her morals were far more loose than Samantha's had ever been, but in spite of all that, she had yet to win his heart the way Miss Martens had.

"The movies? Aww, there's nothing good playing tonight," Gary said, leading her around a corner. His mind was still preoccupied with his afternoon ride with Crane and subsequent invitation to join him and help out at the drag races the following day. He felt like the luckiest kid in town. "No good movies at King's Cinema, anyway..."

She looked puzzled. "Where, then?"

"Skyway."

"The drive-in? But we don't even have a car."

"Who said you need a car?"

"Umm... *'drive'* in..."

"Ha. I prefer to call it *'sneak'* in..." The jeep's clutch disc was going to empty his piggy bank; he had just enough money to buy them some popcorn and a soda to share.

"Oh... You're going to make me break the law, huh?" She laughed.

"You know you love it. There's a perfect spot up on the hill to watch from. Nice and private..." He shot her a knowing smile.

"Hmm... Sounds... perfect," she purred, snaking her arm around his waist.

Gary turned his attention back to the slowly dwindling street lamps. "Jane Rockwell, you're a bad girl. My Granny warned me about dames like you."

"Ha, ha. You love me."

That statement made Gary bristle slightly, but he quickly squelched the feeling and kissed her. He'd rather lie to her and get some action than go home and just think about it, having learned that being truthful with girls about how he truly felt was a real joy kill. So he'd started letting them believe whatever they wanted. Sure, it made him feel like a heel, but it was a sacrifice he was willing to make.

"This *is* nice..." Jane said, settling down on a fallen tree. Through a break in the otherwise thick foliage, they had a perfect view of the massive movie screen below. "Do you come here often?"

"Sure, I bring girls here all the time," he said, smiling.

"You'd better not..."

"Okay, wait here," he said, starting down the hill, "I'll go get us some eats."

"Hurry back. I might get cold," she called to him.

"It'd be better if you got hot... Hold tight. I'll be right back." He high-stepped his way down the grassy hillside and unto the gravel parking lot, which was packed to capacity with cars full of film-goers, some of whom he recognized as rowdy teenagers who obviously had no interest in watching Demetrius and his Gladiators. The pulsing light of the screen guided him to the small, white concessions stand at the rear of the lot.

"Well, well, well... if it ain't The Lonely Wolf," the young man behind the counter said.

"Very funny, Jude..." Gary reached into his pocket. "Gimme a small popcorn and a Coke. Two straws."

"Who do ya got up on the hill with you tonight? Marilyn Monroe?"

"Maybe I do. Wouldn't you like to know."

"Hey. I'd be careful if I was you; I could blow the

whistle on your little hilltop escapades if I wanted to. That'll be twenty five cents..."

Gary slapped a quarter down on the counter. "And *I* could break every bone in your body if I wanted to, so I guess that makes us even." He snatched up his purchases. "See you around, Judas."

"Yeah, enjoy the picture, Romeo."

As he was walking back to the hill behind a row of cars, he spotted her, sitting in a convertible Chevy with Roger Newhawk. He'd recognize that sun-streaked, walnut brown ponytail anywhere. It was Samantha, leaning on Roger's shoulder. A searing pain shot through his insides. It was the first time he'd seen her away from school and with another guy in the eight months since she had left him standing alone in the dark outside of town. What a fool he'd been that night, and burning his old house down was the least of it. If only he could go back, he thought, and then he remembered Grandpa Roy's words about the past. It was over. Done with. He had no choice but to move on. Jane was waiting for him at the top of the hill, and she had the tools and skills to make him forget Samantha Martens. At least until morning.

Sunday, June 27th

Gary could scarcely sit still during the church service. His mind was abuzz with images of burning rubber and chrome, with sounds of squealing tires and roaring engines. Reverend Weaver was saying something that had to do with the Bible. That's all he was sure of. He glanced at his grandmother's watch. Five minutes to go. He trained his eyes on the second hand, which seemed to be ticking in slow motion. Come *on*, he thought, just take our money already.

Finally, the collection plate was passed around and the closing prayer was said, after which he immediately jumped up from his seat on the pew.

"Bye, guys," he burst out to his grandparents.

"Now, wait a minute... hold your horses," Roy said. "Here... here's some lunch money." He handed Gary a dollar.

"What time will you be home, dear?" Kate asked.

"Thanks, Gramps... I don't know. Crane's gonna bring me home after the race is over. It might be late. He's supposed to pick me up here at ten sharp, so I gotta get goin'." He had already begun to unbutton his dress shirt.

"Okay..." Kate said, sounding worried. "Be careful. Those hot-rodders aren't nice boys like you."

Oh, if you only knew, Grandma, he thought to himself. If you only knew... "Okay. I'll be careful. I'll see you guys later... Don't wait up." With that, he bolted from the sanctuary, through the foyer, and out into the blazing morning sunlight. Crane was already waiting for him, smoking as he leaned against the roadster, decked out in his usual attire.

"'Bout time, kid," he said. He flicked the cigarette butt away and jumped into the car.

"Sorry, Crane. I heard you pull up." Gary slid in beside him.

Crane brought the engine to life. "Yup. This little honey's chompin' at the bit to go kick some ass. You ready?"

"You bet I am! Punch it!" An uncontrollable grin stretched across Gary's face as Crane laid into the accelerator, spewing gravel and dirt across the entire church parking lot.

As they crested the final hill coming out of Willowgrove, the new drag strip spread out before them, its shiny black quarter-mile line completely surrounded by hundreds of glittering, shimmering, sparkling speed machines. Gary gasped in awe. No monument on earth would have impressed him more. The very field itself seemed to be one giant, chrome plated, spit-shined sun catcher.

"Wow..." he exclaimed.

Crane began downshifting. "Looks like we made it just in time. Told ya it was gonna be big stuff." He turned left onto the dusty gravel driveway and slowed to a stop as someone resembling an official waved at him.

"Racing or spectating?" the man asked.

"Brother," Crane replied, "I don't even know what spectatin' means, see?"

"Okay, racing, then." The man pulled out a clipboard and began writing. "Name?"

"King Crane McCall... Yeah, and this here's my crew, Lone Wolf, see?" He jabbed his thumb at Gary.

Gary smiled, feeling important. The joy and excitement was building up inside of him like a pop bottle in a paint shaker.

"Roadster class?" the man asked.

"Sounds about right."

"Alright, fellas... sign here." He handed the clipboard to Crane, who chicken scratched his name and passed it to Gary.

He signed it 'Lone Wolf', since that was how he'd been introduced.

"Alright, best of luck to you," the man said, retrieving the clipboard. "You can pull right up there on the left and follow that road. You can pit in the grass there."

"Okay, thanks, Mack. When do we get to run?"

The official looked at his watch. "Time trials start in about ten minutes."

"Cool. Thanks." Crane eased the clutch out and began rolling toward the field.

Gary's eyes could scarcely take everything in; from the innumerable about of sedans, coupes, roadsters and hodge-podge, race-only machines, to the droves of colorful-looking characters that milled in and about the cars. There were hot rodders, obviously, but also greasers, preps and family men, red and yellow, black and white. It seemed like every demographic of American male had been united together under the checkered flag. And, of course, there were the girls; young, old, pretty and plain. A few of the ladies even appeared to be preparing to pilot machines of their own down the quarter mile.

"Nice..." Crane said, pointing to a particularly eye-catching, red-headed female wiping the dust from her new Buick. "I'm goin' huntin' for that little fox before the sun goes down."

"Yeah... she's somethin'... But I already got a girl."

"Well, she ain't here now, is she? I got *three* chicks..."

"Actually, I invited her to come out here after she gets outta church."

"Better work fast, then, kid! Just look at all these lovely, lonely baby machines..."

Gary laughed. "Baby machines? I guess that's *one* way to look at 'em..."

Crane swung into an empty pit spot. "Listen, kid. When it comes to chicks, you gotta treat 'em like toys. Otherwise, every single, bloodsuckin' one of 'em'll break your precious little heart into a billion little bits, trust me. You can't care too less." He shut the car off and then leaned closer to Gary, lowering his voice, as if passing down some ancient, secret wisdom. "And it works this way, too: actin' like you don't give a damn about 'em makes 'em want you even more, see? Chicks always dig most what they think they can't have, see?"

"Oh..." Gary wondered what sort of woman it had taken to give Crane such a sour view of the female race. Perhaps he'd met Candice.

Crane leaned back and opened his door. "Now, you just keep that little pineapple tidbit under your hat. I don't share my hard fought secrets with e'ryone."

"Got it," Gary said, crossing his heart. He wasn't sure if Crane's advice was solid, but he filed it away in the back of his mind, just in case.

"My ears are ringing!" Jane yelled over the raspy roar of a pair of roadsters leaving the line, tires smoking. "Why do we have to stand so close?"

Gary ignored her. He had found his passion. After an entire day of standing mere feet away from the starting line, his ears were ringing, as well, but he didn't care, nor did he mind the nostril-burning aromas of hot rubber and raw fuel that were engulfing him. He watched the cars disappear down the drag strip and then turned his attention back to the line. "Here he comes!" he said, pointing to Crane's hot rod, which was lining up against a quick-looking, flat black roadster. He watched as Crane adjusted his sunglasses against the low sun, and then pulled his leather driving gloves tight. A lit cigarette dangled from his lips. He's so cool, Gary thought. He couldn't think of a more masculine image than Crane, decked out in leather, shoulders hunched, gloved fingers curling tightly around the steering wheel of the most wicked machine he'd ever laid eyes on. He wanted to be just like him.

"I'm tired... How many more people does he have to race?"

Gary rolled his eyes. "If he wins this one, he's gonna be in the final round." He watched as Crane eased his roadster up to the starting line, eyes trained on the green flag in the starter's hand. The RPMs came up. The flag flew. The roadsters shot forward in a blur, quickly running through their gears and disappearing down the quarter mile. Gary held his breath, waiting for the flag man at the end of the race track to signal the winner. The checkered flag fell to the left lane. "Yeah!" Gary exclaimed, grabbing Jane's arm and shaking her. "He's on a roll! C'mon, let's go see if he needs anything!"

"Shit, shit, *shit!*" Crane yelled, violently kicking the roadster's door shut.

Startled, Gary slowed from his jog and released Jane's hand. "What? What's wrong?"

Crane shook his head. "She's busted! I got no clutch!" He threw his gloves into the car. "God*dammit!* I was goin' to the final!"

Gary's mind raced, trying to find a solution. "What broke? What part?"

"Who the hell knows... Feels like the linkage or somethin'... Felt it when I shifted into third... *Shit!*" He collapsed on the ground, cradling his head in his hands.

"Uh..." Gary thought for a moment. "You know how to drive without a clutch?"

Crane looked at him like he'd just stepped out of a UFO. "Huh?"

"Without a clutch. Have you ever driven that way?"

"What the hell are you talkin' about, kid? You can't drive without a clutch!"

Gary's mind flew back to the previous afternoon, when he and Frank had been forced to drive the limping jeep back to the hangar without the use of its clutch pedal.

"Yes you can. I know how."

"Are you for real? You're like thirteen!"

"Fifteen. I've been driving since I was twelve. I'm tellin' you, you can drive without a clutch if you have to."

Crane shook his head. "You're crazy, kid. She's busted. And we got no time or parts to fix her."

As if to punctuate Crane's statement, a call came over the loud speaker for all finalists to return to the starting line.

Gary pondered something for a moment. What did he have to lose? "Let me drive her."

"What?" Crane gave him another 'you must be from another planet' look.

Gary crouched down to eye level with him. "What can it hurt? You want that trophy? I can get it for you." He tried to sound a bit more confident than he actually was.

"Listen, kid, I appreciate ya trying to help out, but... ain't nobody ever drives this rod but me. You don't even have a driver's license, right?"

"It's already broke. I'm not gonna hurt her any more than she already is. I'm tellin' you, I know what I'm doing. If you can push me to the line, I can win this race for you. Think about it. Bein' the first guy to win the first race here... Pretty big stuff."

Crane was silent, staring blankly into the grass. Finally, he said, "You're not supposed to switch drivers."

That sounded like an in route to Gary. "Gimme your sunglasses. And your jacket. You're not much taller than me. Nobody'll know the difference."

After a long moment, Crane took a deep breath and growled, shaking his head again. He looked at Gary and pursed his lips.

Gary held his breath, silently praying for a chance.

Crane ripped his jacket off. "Screw it. Keys are in the ignition."

Gary's heart was about to pound a hole through his chest as he slipped his old ace of spades good luck card behind the speedometer bezel. His breath came hard. Sweat trickled off of his forehead and into his eyes. He had to keep reminding himself that he wasn't dreaming as he wobbled the tall shifter back and forth and brought the engine to life. He could do this, he kept telling himself.

"Ready?" Crane yelled from behind the car.

Gary gave him a thumb up and felt the roadster slowly creep forward. He glanced at his opposition in the right lane. It was a nasty-looking little hot rod with a sneering devil painted on the driver's door, taunting him. His eyes trained back on the flag man. He pressed down on the gas pedal, bringing the engine off of its idle. This was it. He tightened his fingers around the steering wheel, just as he'd seen Crane do. The instant the flag flew, he rammed the shifter into first gear with all of his strength and the roadster lurched forward, grinding Gary into the seat with more force than he'd ever felt in his life. He didn't even have a moment to look to his right before it was time to shift. Jerking backward on the stick, he forced the transmission to accept second gear under full load. The devil roadster was beginning to fall behind. The gravity against him was so great that he felt like he was hanging from the steering wheel. Third gear. Jamming it forward, the shift knob vibrated violently beneath his hand, fighting against him. It didn't appreciate what he was trying to accomplish. He felt the roadster begin to slow. Not good. His opposition was closing in. With every ounce of force that he could muster, he hammered third gear into place. The end of the track was closing in; the devil staring him straight in the eyes. It was going to be close. Too close for him to call. The finish line streaked by in a blur beneath him.

He let off of the accelerator and stomped on the brakes, trying to find the win flag behind him in the rear view mirror, but the end of the track was rough and bumpy, and the mirror rendered useless by the jostling. He continued to slow and then eased the shifter out of third and back into first as he pulled off of the drag strip. He glanced at the man in the devil rod, who shrugged, clearly unsure of the winner himself.

"Holy *Moses*," Gary exclaimed to himself, trying to catch his breath. Win or lose, it was the most exhilarating thing he'd ever done. "What a ride!" If he died right then, he thought, he'd die the happiest young man on earth.

The hot rod shuddered to a stop as he swung it back into its pit spot. Gary let out a deep breath. He thought he was hooked before, but now he knew that there would be no turning back; this would become his addiction, his drug of choice. He was now officially a speed junkie. His thoughts were interrupted by wild yelling coming from behind him. He turned to see Crane, arms spread wide and a look of pure, unadulterated joy plastered on his face.

"Yeah! Yeah!" he continued to bellow as he ran.

Gary hopped out of the car and was nearly bowled over as Crane wrapped his arms around him and lifted his feet off of the ground.

"You did it, kid! *You did it!*"

"R-really?" Gary exclaimed, barely able to speak through Crane's crushing bear hug. He couldn't believe his ears.

"Yeah, really!" Crane sat him down and cupped his hands on Gary's face. "I ain't never, an' I mean *never*, seen *anything* like that in my life! That was beautiful, kid, just *beautiful!*"

Jane soon caught up and leapt for Gary, wrapping her arms around his neck and kissing him with such force that he nearly fell over for a second time. "Oh, baby!" she said, pulling back. "That was incredible!"

"I guess so..." Gary said, still unable to believe it.

Crane slapped him on the back. "Boy, are we gonna celebrate tonight!"

"Celebrate?" Gary asked.

"Yeah, buddy!" Crane walked to the trunk of the roadster and popped it open, revealing three cases of Budweiser.

"What the...? You mean that was in there the whole time?"

"Yup!"

"Well, no wonder she never spun the tires!" Gary laughed, leaning against the hot rod. He heard the last pair of cars run down the track. What a day, he thought. What a beautiful day.

"Have another one, champ!" Crane said, handing Gary a beer after popping the cap. "You earned it!"

Gary accepted it, even though his head was already swimming from the previous five. The sun had finally sunk behind the hills and the little group that had formed around Crane's car were blanketed in its orange afterglow. Someone had gathered a few nearby branches and started a small fire. With Jane still hanging onto him, Gary sat on the ground, gazing into the flames with exhausted joy.

Crane settled down against his roadster. He was cradling the trophy in his arms like a newborn baby. "An' ya know..." he said, slightly slurring his words, "you earned this, too..." He held out the glittering trophy.

Gingerly, Gary took it. It was gorgeous, reading: *'Inaugural Blossom County Dragway Roadster Class*

Winner, June 27, 1954'. More beautiful than any girl he'd ever seen. "Gee, Crane..." He wanted to keep it more than anything, but he'd promised to the contrary. "I can't keep this. Your car, your trophy."

"Now, now..." Crane held up his hand. "You won that race against all the odds. I insist. If it wasn't for you, we'd all be sittin' at home depressed, see? You gotta deserve somethin' for that."

Gary thought for a moment. "Tell you what... I'll trade you this trophy... for this..." He tugged at Crane's leather jacket, which he'd never removed.

"Done, son," Crane said, laughing. "I got a dozen'a those at home. You can even have the gloves, too. How's about *that?*"

"Cool..." Gary said. "Well, I think I'd better get goin'..."

"Right!" Crane said, pulling himself up by the door handle. "Thanks to our friendly neighborhood hot-rodders here, we got a clutch again..."

"You don't have to take me home, Crane. I can walk into town and call my Grandpa. I don't wanna cut your celebration short. Besides, I gotta walk Jane home, anyways." He was more than a little nervous about his grandparents finding out that he'd been drinking, and figured walking might help the buzz wear off a bit.

"Nonsense, crazy man," Crane said, waving him off. "I'll drive you kids." He looked at Jane. "Where do you live, sweetie pie?"

"Just up the hill... in Willowgrove," Jane replied.

"Willagrove? Well, that's just up the hill! C'mon, we'll drop you off..."

Gary glanced at Jane, but she was too plastered to care how she got home.

"C'mon," Crane prompted, "I'll take you home, an' then I'm gonna go out an' find me that redhead we saw...

Remember that redhead, kid?"

"Yeah," Gary nodded.

"I'm'a gonna find that baby doll an' show her how baby dolls is made..."

Gary helped Jane stand. "Your pop is gonna be pissed," he said, wrapping her arm around his neck to steady her. "Don't you tell him *I* got you drunk..."

"Oh, I'll be fine..."

"That's the spirit!" Crane yelled, bringing the engine to life. "C'mon, champ!" He motion for Gary to get in. "Let's wake the neighbors!"

Gary awoke face down in the middle of a newly-planted cornfield, feeling like someone was pounding on his head with a sledgehammer. "What in the world...?" he wondered out loud, trying to stand. The six beers and several shots of whiskey on an empty stomach had finally caught up with him; his legs wobbled beneath him and he doubled over and threw up. As he pulled off one of his new leather gloves and wiped his mouth, he was surprised to see blood come off on his hand. "What the hell?" he exclaimed softly. Had he drank so much that his insides were bleeding? He wiped again. More blood. Much more. He soon realized that it wasn't coming from inside, but from his face. Running his palm across his forehead resulted in a slick, red hand, completely covered in oozing blood. "What the...?" Then he smelled something burning. He spun around as fast as his impaired equilibrium would allow and saw smoke rising from the base of a large tree about twenty feet away.

Stumbling closer revealed the source of the burning;

it was Crane's roadster, completely engulfed in flames. Panic instantly gripped him. He began to run. Crane was still inside. Gary could make out his form through the blaze, slumped over the broken windshield, his arms and head dangling into the fiery engine compartment.

"Oh, God..." Gary said. He stumbled to the driver's side. The inferno was nearly unbearable. "Crane!" he yelled. Still wearing the leather jacket and one glove, he reached into the flames and dragged Crane the rest of the way out of the car, dropping him in the freshly plowed soil and rolling him over onto his back. But he knew immediately that it was too late; Crane was no longer recognizable. The hellish fire had reduced his arms, face and chest to nothing more than a charred corpse, with bits of skull and bone visible through his sizzling skin. He was long gone.

"Oh, God..." Gary said again. "Oh, no... No, not you..." He fell to his knees and began weeping. This wasn't right, he thought. He must be dreaming. Kings weren't supposed to die like this.

The clock on Gary's nightstand tick-tocked its way past 3:00am. It was obvious that he wouldn't be getting any sleep that night. Every time he closed his eyes, the image of Crane's flayed, flame-eaten face hung in the darkness like a ghost that just wouldn't go away. It sickened him that an entire life of dreams and desires, of guidance and inspiration, could be cut short so suddenly and with such violence. Nobody was safe from the Reaper's sickle, not even his heroes.

A rattling sound came from the window, startling

him. The silhouette of a cat filled the pane. It was only Charlie.

Struggling against his aching frame, Gary climbed out of bed and pushed up the screen, letting her in. "Hey, baby girl..." he said softly, running his hand down her back. She began purring. "Come on." He crawled back into bed gingerly; the movement made his head throb. Charlie pounced from the window sill and tip-toed her way onto Gary's chest, her favorite sleeping spot. He began petting her.

Her purr grew louder as she stretched her limbs and laid down.

"Did you miss me, huh, girl?" As he rubbed her furry belly, he wondered how the community would take the news in the morning. Though he knew the general population would chalk it up to another drunken, reckless hot rodder getting what he deserved, he had admired Crane his whole life. His entire character could be summed up in one word: fearless -- and that's exactly how Gary wanted to live and love and be. Sometimes it seemed like an insurmountable task. Fear had so many faces.

He sighed deeply, wincing at the pain in his lungs, as his eyes were drawn across the room to the back of the door, where his new, fire-singed leather jacket hung. To him, it represented much more than just an article of clothing. It was a mantle, a symbol, a reminder. And although the sleeves were a little too long, and the shoulders a bit too broad, he determined to fill them out, even if it took him to his dying breath...

To be continued in...

The Ballad of Carson Creek - The Lone Wolf
Part II : The Carson Valley Kid

Visit: balladofcarsoncreek.com *for up-to-date news!*

Made in the USA
Middletown, DE
07 January 2016